The

North Hollywood

Detective Club

In

The Case of the Dead Man's Treasure

Mike Mains

Chapter 1

A graveyard at midnight is a scary place, and seems even scarier when forced at gunpoint to dig your own grave. With each shovelful of dirt he extracted from the earth, Jeffrey Jones knew that he and his friends were one step closer to their deaths.

He shot a look at his best friend, Pablo, digging alongside of him and not betraying an ounce of fear. Crazy, heroic Pablo, loyal to the end. Would his life be snuffed out at the age of fourteen?

He stole a glance at the two girls, Marisol and Susie, standing over the makeshift grave, flashlights in hand. They were shivering, not from the cold, biting wind, but from the knowledge that death was imminent.

"That's enough," said the man, his voice cutting like a knife across the silent cemetery. He waved his gun at the girls. "Get in the hole."

Marisol gasped. Susie began to whimper.

Jeffrey's heart thumped against his chest and his mind raced. If only he hadn't gotten them all into this mess. His friends were about to die and it was all his fault. He and Pablo dropped their shovels. The tools hit the earth with a dull thud. The girls stepped into the hole.

"You can't kill me," Susie sniveled. "I have a math test

tomorrow!"

"Shut up." The man fixed Jeffrey with a deadly stare. "You are a fat and clever boy, but now your time is up. Say goodbye to your friends." He sneered and raised his gun....

Two Weeks Earlier

"Rubbish! Absolute rubbish!"

Mr. Herbert E. Beasley spoke with a clipped British accent to his ninth grade English class at Trinity High School. He held a paper gingerly between his thumb and forefinger, pinky extended, as if it were a foul-smelling rag, and dropped the offending item on the desk of Jeffrey Jones.

Jeffrey stared at the paper and blinked his pale blue eyes. It was warm in Mr. Beasley's class, always warm, and Jeffrey's owl-shaped glasses had slid down to the tip of his nose. His hands were sweaty and they smudged the red F emblazoned across the top of his paper. "What's rubbish about it?" he asked, still staring at the paper.

"Why it's disgraceful!" Mr. Beasley snatched the paper off Jeffrey's desk and marched to the front of the room. "Your first question was: 'What do the following three words – peep, pop, and refer – all have in common?' The correct answer: they are all verbs. Your answer: 'They are all spelled the same way forwards and backwards.' "

There was a chuckle from the class and a rustle of papers as everyone checked the words to see if that was true.

Jeffrey blushed a deep crimson and squirmed in his seat.

He was a stocky boy and the wooden desk creaked under his weight.

Mr. Beasley continued. "Next question: 'What do the following three words – gum, rats, and spoons – all have in common?' The correct answer: they are all one syllable nouns. Your answer: 'Each of these words forms another word when spelled backwards.' "

Another chuckle and another rustle of papers. Jeffrey shrank deeper into his desk, wishing he could disappear.

Sitting across the aisle from Jeffrey, Pablo Reyes gripped his desk tightly and stared back at Mr. Beasley, his brown eyes burning with indignation.

Mr. Beasley stood taller before the class. "Last question: 'What do the following four words – banana, dresser, grammar, and potato – all have in common?' The correct answer: they are all multi-syllable nouns. Your answer, Mr. Jones: 'Moving the first letter of each word to the end of the word creates the same word spelled backwards.' "

The class burst into laughs. Mr. Beasley smiled triumphantly before them. Jeffrey stared at the floor, his face flaming.

Pablo raised his hand. He was a muscular boy and when he spoke, people listened. "Excuse me, Mr. Beasley, but Jeffrey's answers are correct."

"How dare you!"

"But they are," Pablo insisted. "That's just the way Jeffrey thinks. He can't help it if he's a genius."

The class howled with laughter.

Jeffrey covered his face with his hands.

Mr. Beasley stared back at Pablo, the interloper. "A genius, is he? At fourteen-years-old?"

"It's true," said Marisol Rodriguez, a pretty girl, with light brown skin and long black hair. Pablo glanced at Marisol, but she pretended not to notice. She swept her hair away from her face, and kept her big oval eyes focused on Mr. Beasley.

"Is that so?" said Mr. Beasley. "Let me tell you something, all of you. I'll not be upstaged by a student with the wrong answers. Jones, your grade is an F!" He sat down behind his desk with a huff.

"Don't feel bad, Mr. Beasley," Pablo said. "Jeffrey is smarter than lots of adults."

Mr. Beasley slammed Jeffrey's paper down on his desk. The paper made no noise, it was his fist that landed with a resounding crack and silenced the room. Two dozen young faces ducked and stared down at their desks.

Jeffrey raised his hand. "Mr. Beasley, I'm sorry. I thought I answered the questions correctly."

"You did answer them correctly," Pablo said.

"That's enough," snapped Mr. Beasley. He fixed Jeffrey with a withering stare. "Comedian, eh?"

"No, sir."

"Let me tell you something, Mr. Jones. And you, Mr.

Reyes. I heard all about your little adventure over the summer. Detective club, indeed." Mr. Beasley placed his hands firmly on the armrests of his chair and rose up before the class. "I'll have you know that you're not dealing with a two-bit actress and her collection of second-rate art thieves."

Mr. Beasley cast a simmering look at each of the two boys. He had read in the newspaper and heard from other teachers about the case of the Hollywood art heist that Jeffrey and Pablo had solved over the summer. The boys had rescued Marisol's brother from jail and even solved a 20-year-old murder. Mr. Beasley was not impressed. "I am Herbert E. Beasley," he said, "and I have graded your paper as I see fit: an F!"

He flung Jeffrey's paper across the room. It fluttered through the air and landed on the floor in the back of the classroom. A kid kicked it, then another, and another. The paper, now covered in scuff marks, ended on the floor in front of Jeffrey's desk.

Jeffrey placed a finger on the center of his glasses and pushed them back up his nose. "I'd like to appeal my grade."

Mr. Beasley's eyes narrowed into slits. "Appeal? What do you mean appeal?"

"Like they do in court."

The class snickered.

"And to whom do you intend to submit this appeal?"

"To the principal."

"And just what makes you think that the principal of this school has time for your petty grade?"

"It's not petty to me."

"Nonsense."

"I've never had an F before."

"Well, you do now. We will not disturb the principal of this school with such a trifling matter. The subject is closed." He turned to the blackboard, snatched up a piece of chalk, and began writing the week's assignment. The chalk made shrill staccato squeaks against the blackboard.

"It's not fair, Mr. Beasley."

"I'll be the judge of that."

"But it's my permanent record. My permanent record is ruined."

The chalk in Mr. Beasley's hand snapped in half against the blackboard. He spun around and faced Jeffrey. "Enough with you and your permanent record! You think you know everything, don't you? You think you can outsmart me, is that it?"

"No, sir."

Mr. Beasley dusted the chalk off his hands. "You most certainly do. Very well, if that's the way you want it, we will play your little game. I will give you a chance – just one chance, mind you – to improve your grade."

Jeffrey blinked. What was his teacher up to?

A thin smile crept over Mr. Beasley's face. "I will present

you with a question of logic, a mystery, if you will. Your answer will be timed. Sixty seconds. If you are successful in solving it, I shall change your grade to an A. If not, then you will accept the grade I have given you, and the subject will be closed. Do you accept my challenge?"

Heads turned, all eyes were on Jeffrey.

Jeffrey glanced at Pablo.

"Don't look at him for the answer," said Mr. Beasley.

"Don't do it, Jeffrey," Pablo whispered. "It's a trap."

Jeffrey turned to Marisol.

"Don't look at her, either."

Marisol stared back at Jeffrey with wide-open eyes and shook her head.

Mr. Beasley folded his arms across his chest. "Well?"

Jeffrey looked up at Mr. Beasley and took a deep breath. "I accept."

The class burst into clamor. Bodies shifted. Desks thumped and scraped against the floor to give their occupants a better view of Jeffrey and the teacher.

"Silence!" Mr. Beasley commanded. "If anyone supplies the answer, it will result in immediate disqualification."

The class quieted.

Mr. Beasley unbuttoned his suit jacket. He hooked a thumb under the armpit of his wool vest. With his free hand, he removed a timepiece attached to a small gold chain from the watch pocket on his vest. He looked up and fixed Jeffrey with a steely gaze.

"They tell me you can solve any mystery. Very well, solve this. A man enters a pub and asks the bartender for a glass of water. The bartender removes a revolver from under the bar and points it at the man. Surprised, the man says, 'Thank you,' and leaves the pub. Explain their behavior. You have sixty seconds." He checked the time on his watch.

The room was silent, save for the soft electric hum of the clock on the wall. The class sat perfectly still, barely breathing. All eyes were on Jeffrey.

Jeffrey stared at his desk. Pablo watched with a growing sense of panic. The puzzle was impossible. Nobody could solve it. He turned to Marisol. She watched Jeffrey with a shaken look on her face. Her brown eyes looked moist and ready to cry.

"Fifty seconds," said Mr. Beasley.

Jeffrey squirmed in his seat. In the quiet of the classroom, the groan of his desk was as loud as a shout.

"Forty-five seconds."

Jeffrey continued to stare at his desk.

Mr. Beasley made no effort to conceal his delight. "A simple question of logic, Mr. Jones. A man walks into a pub.... Surely, a genius of your repute can rise to the challenge. Tick tock, tick tock."

Jeffrey frowned. The entire class watched him, but he seemed not to know they were even there.

"Thirty-five seconds."

"Come on, Jeffrey!" Pablo whispered.

"No encouragement!"

Jeffrey rose and walked slowly to the window. The class leaned forward as one, following him with their eyes. Pablo's knuckles turned white as he gripped his desk. The clock ticked.

"Twenty seconds."

Jeffrey stared out the window.

"Fifteen seconds!"

"I need more time."

"Ten seconds!"

A girl shrieked with tension. Another screamed.

"Five seconds!"

"Mr. Beasley, it's not fair!" Marisol cried.

"Three seconds!"

Jeffrey suddenly straightened up.

"Time!"

"Hiccups," Jeffrey said.

Marisol gasped. The class froze.

Jeffrey turned to Mr. Beasley. "The man who entered the pub had the hiccups. The bartender recognized this from the man's speech and because he asked for a glass of water. The bartender pointed the gun at the man to shock him out of his hiccups. It worked and the man said, 'Thank you.' That's the answer."

There was a moment of stunned silence, and then the class erupted with thunderous applause and whistles. Mr. Beasley stared back at Jeffrey, the color drained from his face.

A pair of loutish boys in the back of the room began to chant, "Jef-frey! Jef-frey! Jef-frey!" Smiling wide, Pablo and Marisol joined them, and the entire class took up the chant. "Jef-frey! Jef-frey! Jef-frey!" The words shock the classroom. Jeffrey closed his eyes and put a hand over his face.

The bell rang and the class rose like a flock of sparrows, chanting Jeffrey's name and pumping their fists as they marched out of the room. Mr. Beasley sat behind his desk and slumped in his chair, looking like a fighter who'd just gone ten rounds. Marisol ran to Jeffrey and hugged him.

Pablo picked Jeffrey's paper up from the floor and put his arm around his friend's shoulder. As they passed Mr. Beasley's desk, Pablo handed him Jeffrey's paper. "No hard feelings, huh, Mr. Beasley?" Pablo said.

Mr. Beasley snatched the paper from Pablo's hand. Frowning, he picked up a red pen, crossed out the letter F, and replaced it with a large letter A. He thrust the paper back at the boys. "Indeed," he said.

Chapter 2

As he drove home that evening, Mr. Beasley replayed the day's events in his mind. Fourteen years of teaching and he'd never been bested by a student, until today.

Just who was this portly boy named Jeffrey Jones? Where had he come from? And how the devil had he managed to solve that riddle? No one had ever solved that riddle! Not even he, Herbert E. Beasley, could solve that riddle.

He jerked the steering wheel and spun the car dangerously around a turn. Better slow down, he told himself. He was letting his emotions get the better of him, and that was something he never allowed. But how could he possibly concentrate?

Humiliated by a student, a freshman, no less. Disgraceful! He could still hear that infernal chant in his head: "Jef-frey! Jef-frey! Jef-frey!" It was stuck in his mind like an obnoxious song he'd heard on the radio and couldn't shake, playing over and over and over. He banged his fist on the dashboard.

The other teachers had warned him. They told him not to challenge the boy's intellect. But he didn't listen. He slowed the car and eased to a stop at a red light. Drumming his fingertips along the top of the steering wheel, he considered his situation. There was only one recourse open to him now, and it was a matter of honor. He would find a way to outsmart Jeffrey Jones and regain the upper hand if it was the last thing he did. And he would do it in spectacular fashion.

The light ahead of him turned green. He took his foot off the brake and accelerated slowly into the intersection. He was smiling now. He had his solution and nothing could go wrong.

A car horn blared in his ear. He turned to see an old unwashed Porsche, gray and squat like a German army helmet, running the red light and barreling towards him.

He jammed the brake pedal and spun the wheel. The Porsche slammed into his car. Glass exploded. Metal screamed. His body, encased in a seatbelt, slapped forward and then back.

In a moment, it was over. He slumped in his seat, gazing upward through the smoke that poured from the hood of his car. He smelled oil and gasoline and burnt tire rubber.

An engine revved. He twisted his throbbing neck to see the Porsche, its front fender hanging by a thread, skidding backwards. The car screeched to a stop, shifted into drive, and raced off, its dangling metal fender scraping along the pavement.

"What happened?" he moaned, just before he passed out.

Chapter 3

Whispers and rumors spread like wildfire through the halls and classrooms at school.

"Did you hear about Mr. Beasley?"

"No, what?"

"He got run over by a car yesterday."

"No way! For real?"

"That's what I heard."

"Nah, man, it wasn't a car, it was a truck."

"A truck?"

"One of those big tractor trailers you see on the freeway."

"That can't be right."

"What can't be right?"

"He says Beasley got hit by a truck."

"He didn't get hit by a truck, he fell off a cliff."

"That's crazy!"

"I'm telling you."

"Where'd you hear that?"

"Everyone knows it."

"Is he dead?"

"He's gotta be dead."

"Beasley ain't dead. He's in the hospital. His house burned down."

"Get outa here!"

"I'm serious. It got hit by lightning. Beasley was fried to a crisp."

"Nah, man. He drowned."

"Drowned?"

"That's what everyone is saying."

"I heard it was an ax murderer. Chopped off his head."

"Yuck!"

"Here comes Jeffrey and Pablo, let's ask them!"

Jeffrey and Pablo approached from down the hall. A gang of kids swarmed over them.

"Did you hear about Beasley? I heard he drowned! I heard he got hit by a car! I heard he fell off a cliff! I heard he got his head chopped off!"

Jeffrey and Pablo looked at each other, and then back at the crowd, gathered in front of them.

"I think you're all crazy," Pablo said.

Chapter 4

"Good heavens, man. My car is destroyed, I was nearly killed, and you tell me there's nothing you can do?"

Mr. Beasley lay sprawled across his sofa at home, two days after the accident. He wore a brace around his neck, his left leg was in a cast, and he sported two black eyes.

His wife, Mildred, sat on the sofa next to him. A uniformed police officer sat in a stiff-backed chair across from them both.

"You don't have the license plate number of the car that hit you," the officer said, "and you don't have any witnesses. Even if you did have the license number, it would take us two weeks to run the plates."

"Two weeks?"

"At least two weeks."

"Preposterous!"

"Calm down, Herbert," Mildred advised.

Mr. Beasley twisted as best he could through his neck brace and looked at his wife. "Don't tell me to calm down. Don't you understand? I've never been in an accident before in my life! Never a speeding ticket! Never a parking ticket! My record is spotless - squeaky-clean spotless - and now this. My permanent record is ruined!" Wait a second, he thought. Where had he heard that before?

"Los Angeles is a big city, sir," the officer said. "A lot of crime. We just don't have the manpower to investigate traffic accidents unless there's a fatality or damage to city property."

"So if I were dead, or if I were a bench in a city park, then you'd investigate, eh?"

"I'm afraid that's true."

Mr. Beasley snorted and looked away.

The officer rose. "You have my card, sir. Call me if you come across any new information."

"Yes, of course, officer," Mildred said. "Thank you." She walked him to the front door.

Mr. Beasley stared out the window at the lemon trees in his front yard. So that's the way it was, eh? Abandoned by all, helped by none. Well, he was Herbert E. Beasley, and though he was down, he was not out. Though he was bent, he was not broken. He had a plan up his sleeve.

He was still staring out the window when his wife returned to the living room. "Well, Herbert," she said, "I suppose we're out of luck. We'll never find the driver who hit you now."

"Nonsense," Mr. Beasley replied, turning his eyes from the window and looking intently at his wife. "If the police can't do their jobs, then there's one person in this city who can."

Mildred stared at him in disbelief. "Why, who could that

be?"

He smiled as he gazed back out the window.

"Jeffrey Jones."

Chapter 5

High school football is a wonderful sport; a game of speed, skill, and chess-like strategy. The Friday afternoon game between the freshman team of Trinity High and St. Ignatius Prep was none of those things.

Played under a drenching rain, it was a muddy, sloppy, grinding mess. St. Ignatius Prep had managed a single, shaky field goal that somehow wobbled its way over the crossbar. Trinity High hadn't even done that. They trailed 0-3, late in the fourth quarter and St. Ignatius Prep had the ball.

Coach Franklin of Trinity High huddled with his team on the sideline under a wall of water. Two dozen mud-splattered faces formed a tight circle around him, their bodies heaving as they gasped for air. "Don't give up!" the coach said. "I know it's hard, I know you're tired, but you've got to keep fighting!"

Blood dribbled from Pablo's nose and a clod of wet turf lay plastered across the bar on his face mask. Next to him, a bulky offensive lineman doubled over, groaning and clutching his side. Pablo steadied his teammate with one arm, and kept his eyes glued on the fiery, granite-jawed coach.

"We're still in this game!" Coach Franklin shouted above the rain. "But we need a stop, and we need to score!"

Behind the sideline, Marisol and the other cheerleaders huddled under a makeshift canopy. A few girls hopped or clapped to keep warm. Marisol, her hair tangled and matted from the rain, surveyed the sideline intently, looking for Pablo in the huddle of players. He had talked about the game all week and she knew how bad he wanted to win.

Behind the cheerleaders, a sprinkling of die-hard fans and family members remained, shouting with hoarse voices at the field.

Mildred Beasley held a soggy newspaper over her head and picked her way carefully through the gathering. She was a small, delicate woman, ill at ease in the pouring rain. Stepping gingerly around a mud puddle, she approached a familiar teacher.

"Hello, Mildred!" the man exclaimed. "What brings you out on a day like this?"

"I'm looking for a student named Jeffrey Jones. Do you know him?"

"Sure, everybody knows Jeffrey. Smartest kid in school. He's over there." The man pointed. Mildred raised up on her tiptoes and squinted through the rain.

Jeffrey huddled underneath a large umbrella with Mrs. Reyes and Pablo's eight-year-old sister, Maria. He was wrapped in a raincoat two sizes too big, and water specks covered his glasses.

Mrs. Reyes stared out at the field with a worried look.

"They're not going to win, are they, Jeffrey?"

Jeffrey didn't answer. It didn't look good for Pablo's team, but he was afraid to admit it.

"They'll win!" Maria said. "Come on, Pablo! Come on!" She clapped her hands.

Coach Franklin looked hard into the eyes of his players. "This is what we practiced for. This is what we worked all summer for. This is the time when winners win and quitters quit. They get another first down and the game's over. I'm counting on all of you. Stay with your assignments. Every man do his job. Win on three." He put his fist out and his tired players laid their hands on top. "One, two – "

"Win!" the players shouted.

Pablo trotted out on the field with the defense and took his position at middle linebacker. Rain pelted his arms and the back of his neck. Under his helmet, raindrops thumped like a soggy jackhammer, drowning his thoughts and water-logging his brain.

Cleats dug in. Bruised and aching bodies crouched into position. The quarterback for St. Ignatius Prep lined up behind center and barked out signals over the downpour. The center snapped the ball.

Flecks of mud flew from the turf. Players lunged, jostled and collided. The quarterback dropped back and rifled the ball. A lanky defensive lineman shot his arms overhead and deflected it. The ball careened upward into the gray, rain-streaked sky.

For Pablo, time seemed to stop. There was no sound. There was no movement. Even the raindrops froze. The ball floated above him and hung in the air.

He leapt and clamped the ball firmly between his hands. For a moment, he seemed to be floating, suspended in midair, and then his feet touched down and a roar of grunts, shouts and popping shoulder pads flooded his ears.

Clutching the ball, Pablo ran. He tore through the line of players in front of him, sidestepping an offensive lineman who dove for his legs. Another lineman grabbed at his jersey and slipped in the muddy turf. The quarterback reached for him and stumbled, grasping at air. Pablo zipped past them all and streaked down the sideline.

The Trinity High sideline exploded with leaps and shouts. Coaches and players pumped their fists and yelled, "Go! Go!"

Marisol and the cheerleaders fanned out from under their canopy and screamed, "Run! Run!"

Jeffrey, Mrs. Reyes, and Maria jumped and hollered, "Go, Pablo! Go!"

Jeffrey felt a tap on his shoulder and turned to see Mildred Beasley blinking up at him. "Are you Jeffrey Jones?"

"Touchdown!" Maria screamed.

Jeffrey turned back to the field. Pablo was in the end zone, being mobbed by his teammates.

Maria shrieked and screamed and grabbed Jeffrey,

yanking on his raincoat and jumping up and down like a wild thing.

"Maria, stop!" yelled Mrs. Rodriguez. But it was too late. Jeffrey lost his balance and stumbled backwards, flailing his arms like an out of control windmill. Further and further he hobbled back, until his knees splayed out and he landed on his seat with a wet plop in a puddle of muddy water.

Mrs. Reyes screamed. Maria laughed and clapped her hands. Mildred Beasley gasped and covered her mouth. Jeffrey sat in the muddy puddle, blinking behind his rain-streaked glasses, and wondering what just happened.

Chapter 6

If Mr. Beasley liked keeping his classroom warm, then his home was twice as bad. Pablo tugged at his collar, and Jeffrey mopped his brow with his sleeve. Both boys wished they'd left their jackets at home.

They were seated in Mr. Beasley's living room. Like the man himself, the furniture in his home was stiff, ornate, and formal. The chairs the boys occupied forced them to sit ramrod straight and the seats were covered in clear plastic vinyl that squished and crinkled under their weight. Each boy had a backpack on the floor by his chair.

Their teacher lay sprawled out on the sofa before them. Although it was early Saturday morning, and despite the fact that he still sported a brace on his neck and a cast on his left leg, Mr. Beasley was impeccably dressed in his customary wool suit and vest. The dark circles under his eyes had cleared considerably, and his face had regained some of its color.

Mildred Beasley sat in a chair by her husband's side, wearing a floral dress. She leaned forward and poured a cup of strong-smelling tea for each of the boys. When she turned her back, Pablo took a sip from his cup and grimaced horribly.

"As you can see, I'm incapacitated," Mr. Beasley said. "If

you're not familiar with that word, it means useless, laid up, unable to move."

"I know what the word means, sir," Jeffrey said.

"You would," Mr. Beasley sighed. "Despite my physical limitations, I am still in possession of man's greatest gift and his most noble faculty: his mind. I can still think. And I am determined to track down the driver who put me in this unenviable position."

"When Mrs. Beasley told us you were in a hit-and-run accident, Pablo and I did some research," Jeffrey said, pulling a manila folder from his backpack.

Mr. Beasley's eyes widened and he sat up as best he could. The vinyl covering on the sofa squeaked under him. He nodded at Jeffrey to continue.

Jeffrey opened the folder and read from a report he and Pablo had prepared. "Los Angeles is the hit-and-run capital of the country with over twenty-thousand hit-and-run accidents a year. Of those, twenty-two bicyclists, forty motorists, and ninety-two pedestrians are killed or badly injured each year. Thousands more are less seriously injured."

"Yes, I'm one of them," Mr. Beasley said. "Continue."

"Most hit-and-run drivers flee the scene, because they are either drunk, unlicensed, or both. Many are convicted felons on early-release parole. Others are living in this country illegally and afraid of deportation. Despite the epidemic of hit-and-run accidents, Los Angeles law enforcement and its political leadership show little interest in investigating any cases that don't involve death or destruction of city property."

"The boy is correct!" Mr. Beasley said excitedly to his wife. "Continue, Jones."

"That's basically it, sir," Jeffrey said, closing the folder. "There's a rash of hit-and-run accidents in this city and no one seems to care."

"Yes, and I am the unfortunate victim. Well, we'll see about that." He cleared his throat and looked Jeffrey in the eye. "I understand you have a detective club."

"Yes, sir," Jeffrey affirmed.

Pablo produced a business card and handed it to Mr. Beasley. The card read:

THE NORTH HOLLYWOOD DETECTIVE CLUB
Investigation and Deductive Reasoning
Senior Detective: Jeffrey Jones
Senior Detective: Pablo Reyes

Mr. Beasley read the card and grunted. "Very well," he said, passing the card to his wife. "I wish to hire you. I want you to find the driver and the car that hit me, and I will pay for your services. Two hundred dollars up front, and an additional two hundred dollars upon delivery of the information I seek. By delivery, I mean the name and address of the driver, or the license plate number of the car." He turned to his wife. "Mildred."

Mildred opened her purse and removed two crisp one hundred dollar bills. Pablo's eyes grew wide at the sight of the money. Mildred handed one bill to each of the boys.

"Thank you!" they both said.

"Unfortunately," said their teacher, "I have little information to provide you. I do not have a license plate number, or a description of the driver. All I know is that the accident occurred last Monday, at precisely four o'clock in the afternoon, and the car that hit me was a gray Porsche. Of that, I am certain. An older model. What year, I cannot tell you. It's also damaged in the front from the accident."

Jeffrey took out a pen and an index card and wrote the information down.

Mr. Beasley looked the two boys over. "I realize it's a seemingly impossible task. Even for you. Still, I cling to the faintest glimmer of hope. Something tells me you just might succeed where the police have failed. Any questions?"

"No, sir," Jeffrey said. "We'll get right on the case."

"Good show. Be on your way then. North Hollywood Detective Club, indeed."

Mildred walked the boys to the front door. Mr. Beasley peaked out from behind the lace window curtains and watched as Jeffrey and Pablo ran to their bikes in the front yard.

"A hundred bucks!" Pablo shouted. "We're rich!"

Mr. Beasley smiled. He had been an industrious boy once himself.

Mildred returned to the living room to find her husband still gazing out the window as the boys pedaled away. "Do you really think they can help, Herbert? After all, they're only boys."

Mr. Beasley turned from the window and gave his wife a knowing smile. "That's what you think."

Chapter 7

The church basement was stacked high with cardboard boxes and canned goods of all kinds. There were racks filled with dresses and overcoats, paintbrushes and paint buckets, bed sheets and pillows, toothpaste, soap, towels, and a table covered with broken toys. The cramped basement room smelled of cardboard, old clothes, and mothballs.

For as long as they could remember, Jeffrey and Pablo had spent a portion of their Saturdays here with Father Pat, who ran the church mission. Today was no different. As they helped the kindly, white-haired priest pack boxes to be shipped to the overseas missions, they told him about Mr. Beasley and the gray Porsche he wanted them to find.

"And he actually paid you?" Father Pat asked, genuinely surprised.

"A hundred bucks," Pablo said. "Each." He pulled the crisp bill that Mildred Beasley gave him from his pocket and showed it to the priest.

Father Pat whistled. "Wish I had a hundred bucks."

"Freshly printed, Father." Pablo held the bill up to his nose and inhaled deeply. "It even smells rich."

Father Pat laughed. "Congratulations, boys. You're professionals now."

"Thanks," Pablo said. "But we don't have a clue how we're

going to find that gray Porsche."

"Not a clue? Not even you, Jeffrey?"

"Not yet, Father," Jeffrey said.

"It's like trying to find a needle in a slaughterhouse, isn't it?" Father Pat mused. He reached for an old stool, pulled it up, and settled himself comfortably, his usual prelude before telling the boys a story. "Which reminds me of the time when I was a young lad in seminary school."

"When was that?" Pablo asked.

"Oh, about a hundred years ago."

The boys laughed.

"We were in quite a pickle then. Seems old Mrs. Jurgens lost her prize cow, Marvel Ann."

"Marvel Ann?" Pablo exclaimed.

"Can you think of a better name for a cow?"

Pablo shrugged.

"Anyway, old Mrs. Jurgens had a farm about five miles from our school and she accused us of making off with Marvel Ann. Now some of the boys at the seminary were up to an occasional prank now and then. Tipping her cows and so forth."

Pablo scratched his head. "Tipping her cows?"

"Cows sleep standing up," Jeffrey put in.

"That's right, Jeffrey," said Father Pat. "So some of the boys would sneak over at night and give one of her sleeping cows a gentle push. But the cows were never hurt, and the boys would never steal anything, much less a cow. But, oh, that Mrs. Jurgens, she knew for a fact that we were guilty and she went straight to the sheriff. And once the sheriff got involved, well, we started believing it ourselves."

"What did you do?" Pablo asked.

"That's a good question, Pablo. How do you lose a cow? And, more importantly, how do you find a cow that's missing? As it just so happened, Mrs. Jurgens was one of the chief contributors to the sheriff's reelection campaign, so when she said, 'Jump', he said, 'How high?' And if she told him we stole Marvel Ann, then, by golly, that sheriff was going to find her.

"In the meantime, while all this hussing and fussing was going on, one of the seminarians thought to himself, this is completely illogical. If Marvel Ann is alive, then she has to be someplace where cows can be fed and housed. You can't keep a cow in a seminary.

"This seminarian told his theory to one of the priests, and the next day the two of them took a drive out to another farm, about fifty miles away. Sure enough, there was old Marvel Ann. The other farmer had stolen her. I remember that incident well, because I was that seminarian. Now I have no idea how that story is going to help you find the car you're looking for, but that's what your problem reminded me of."

"We're the ones in a pickle now," Pablo said.

Father Pat chuckled ruefully and shook his head.

Jeffrey held up a finger. "Actually, Father, you just gave me an idea. If we follow your example of applying logical thought, and ask ourselves what type of person or group of people is more likely to notice a particular model of car. What would the answer be?"

Father Pat shrugged and looked at Pablo.

"I notice cars," Pablo said.

"Exactly," Jeffrey said. "You notice cars, because you can't wait until you're old enough to drive. Neither can I. Neither can any kid our age, especially guys. We've been playing with cars, talking about cars, reading about cars, and dreaming about cars since we were little kids. So to locate a missing car in a city with millions of people and millions of cars, all we have to do is get the word out to guys our age. We'll offer a fifty dollar reward from the money Mr. Beasley gave us to the first person who locates the gray Porsche."

"When you say 'get the word out', you mean on the internet?" Father Pat asked.

"Not directly, because the owner of the car we're looking for might see it. But we can call and send emails and texts to all our friends, and ask all our friends to call and email and text all their friends, and on and on. In a matter of hours, we can have the whole city covered. If an old, banged-up gray Porsche is on the road somewhere in Los Angeles, you can bet a kid our age is going to see it and notice it."

"Jeffrey, it's brilliant!" exclaimed Father Pat.

Jeffrey tilted his head, raised his left eyebrow, and spoke with his best English accent. "On the contrary, it's elementary, my dear Watson. Elementary."

Pablo and Father Pat burst out laughing

Chapter 8

"I want to help!" Marisol cried.

She was with the boys in Jeffrey's basement. The basement served as Jeffrey's bedroom, and it was as messy as Jeffrey's mind was sharp. Books spilled out of Jeffrey's bookcase and covered the floor. There were books piled on top of his desk, books on top of the dresser, even books on Jeffrey's bed. Clothes were draped over chairs or jammed into an open closet. Shoes lay strewn across the floor. Jeffrey sat in a beanbag chair, sunken deep in its contours. Marisol and Pablo sat together on a two-seated sofa, where Jeffrey had cleared a space.

"Do you have any friends who know about cars?" Pablo asked.

"Not really, but my friends have brothers and cousins. Maybe one of them has seen the gray Porsche."

"Sounds good to me," Jeffrey said. "We have a phone down here in the basement, another phone in the kitchen, and my mom's computer in the living room. Who wants what?"

"I'll take the computer and send emails," Marisol said.

"I'll take the phone in the kitchen," Pablo said.

"Great," said Jeffrey. "I'll start calling down here. We'll trade spots in an hour. Everyone ready?" Pablo and Marisol nodded. "On three," Jeffrey said. "One, two, three, go!"

Pablo and Marisol leapt from the sofa and sprinted for the basement stairs. They collided, laughed, and jostled each other as they scrambled up the steps.

"Be careful!" Jeffrey shouted after them. He picked up the phone and dialed. "Hello, Mrs. Edwards? It's Jeffrey. Can I please speak to Bill? ... Hey, Bill, I'm looking for an older model gray Porsche. Have you seen any cars like that? ... It was involved in an accident and I'm trying to track it down. There's a fifty dollar reward for the person who finds it.... Yeah, fifty bucks. Cash.... I *am* serious.... Well, do me a favor, will you? Call all your friends and ask if any of them has seen an older gray Porsche, possibly damaged in front.... Yeah, and don't forget to mention the reward. If one of them finds it, you can split the money with them.... Thanks. Bye." He hung up and made another call.

Upstairs, Marisol typed away on the computer in the living room: *Hey, what's up? Want to make some $$$$? My friend has a $50 reward for anyone who can find an old gray Porsche! Ask your brother! He might know! $$$$!!!! Call me later!*

In the kitchen, Pablo worked the phone: "Yeah, man, it's real. I have the money in my pocket. Fifty bucks if you can find the car.... Call your friends. Whoever finds the car gets the money."

The three of them phoned and emailed for two hours, and

then spent another two hours fielding the flood of tips that came pouring in. Four hours after they began, they reconvened in Jeffrey's basement.

"Chewy Banks says his neighbor has a 1999 blue Porsche," Pablo said. "It's the wrong color, but what if the driver of the gray Porsche had it repainted?"

"Excellent question, Pablo," Jeffrey said. "I hadn't thought about a paint job, but we'll have to consider it. Let's stick with the original gray color for now, but if nothing turns up, we'll pursue the possibility that the driver repainted his car in order to hide it. What else do you have?"

"Hector Gonzalez knows a guy, who knows a guy, whose brother has a gray Porsche, but it's a new car. He just got it a year ago."

"That doesn't sound like the car we're looking for," Jeffrey said, "unless Mr. Beasley was wrong in his description. He did seem pretty sure that it was an older model car."

"Hector also said his dad's boss drives a red Porsche," said Pablo, "and he wants to know if you want to buy his skateboard for twenty bucks."

"I'll pass on the skateboard," Jeffrey said. "How about you, Marisol?"

"I'll pass on the skateboard, too."

"No, I mean about the car."

"Oh. Well, my friend, Gladys, says her cousin saw a gray

Porsche for sale at a car dealership, but it's new. And a girl named Julie Avila, who knows my friend, Gina, says she went out with a guy who drives a Porsche, but it was red and he moved back to San Francisco. And Susie Norris says she doesn't know anything about a gray Porsche, but if you're involved with a new mystery she wants to hear all about it."

Jeffrey frowned. "Susie Norris? Did you have to call her?"

"You said call my friends, and Susie's my friend."

"What did you tell her?"

"Nothing. I said I'd have to ask you."

"Good. The last thing I want is Susie Norris sticking her big nose into this case."

Marisol grinned. "Susie said, 'You tell that Jeffrey Jones he can't keep a secret from me!' And then she asked if you'd lost any weight."

"No, I haven't lost any weight, and yes, I can keep a secret from her."

"You're not going to tell her about the case?" Pablo asked.

"No way. That girl is stuck up."

"That's what she says about you," Marisol said.

"*What?*" Jeffrey nearly fell out of his beanbag chair. "She says *I'm* stuck up?"

"No," Marisol confessed. "But I wanted to see you jump."

Pablo exploded in laughter and pounded his fist on his thigh.

"Very funny!" Jeffrey said, his face flaming red. "Enough

with the jokes."

"What did you come up with, Jeffrey?" Marisol asked.

Jeffrey sifted through half-a-dozen index cards he had made notes on. "Another red Porsche ..." He tossed the card aside. "A black Porsche ..." He tossed that card aside. "A couple of false leads ..." He tossed the cards. "But then Joey Gallagher said he saw a gray Porsche in Sun Valley two days ago with a damaged front end."

"That sounds like our car," Pablo said. He and Marisol both sat up straight.

"Possibly, but Joey doesn't know who it belongs to or where it went." Jeffrey looked at his last index card. "However, I got an email from someone I don't know. A guy named Charlie. He lives in Sun Valley, and he said a man in his neighborhood drives a gray Porsche with a newly damaged front end."

"Is that the same car Joey saw?" Pablo asked.

"Could be."

"But is it the same car we're looking for?" Marisol said.

"We'll find out," Jeffrey said. "We're meeting with Charlie in Sun Valley on Monday."

"I got a feeling that's our car," Pablo said. "It has to be."

"There's only one problem," Jeffrey said. "Charlie wouldn't tell me his last name or where he went to school. And he wouldn't send me a picture of what he looks like."

"What do you think that means?" Marisol asked.

"It means only one of two things. Either Charlie is a very private person, who isn't sure if he can trust us. Or," Jeffrey paused and looked at his friends, "our meeting with him on Monday is a trap."

Chapter 9

On Sunday morning, the three friends all went to church, as was their custom. Pablo's family was especially strict about Sundays. They went to church and then spent the rest of their day together. There was no television allowed on Sundays, no shopping, and no music. In the evening, the family gathered in the living room and took turns reading aloud from the New Testament. Sometimes they prayed the Rosary together. Jeffrey wished his family was as close as Pablo's.

Marisol went to church with her mother and her older brother, Victor. They were a close family, too, although not as strict on Sundays as Pablo's family. Marisol didn't have a father. He had died when she was two-years-old.

Jeffrey's parents were hit and miss with their church attendance, so he usually went alone. Like Pablo and Marisol, and their families, the only church service Jeffrey attended was Father Pat's traditional Latin Mass. Father Pat was an ancient priest, ordained before Vatican II, and he was very strict about upholding traditional Catholic teaching. Father Pat adhered to the traditional consecration of the host, and Communion was given only at the Communion rail, never in the hand. There was no music, no shaking hands with your neighbor, no compromise to modernism at all; just pure adoration of God.

Jeffrey loved it. At Father Pat's Mass, men wore jackets and ties, and women dressed modestly and wore veils over their heads. Stripped from the excesses of the modern service, Jeffrey felt in tune with God at Father Pat's traditional Latin Mass, a participant in a rich and holy tradition dating back two thousand years. It was as if the portals to the supernatural were opened and Heaven revealed in all its majesty.

The solemnity of Father Pat as he said Mass only added to the feeling. Jeffrey didn't understand much of the Latin language, but he had picked up a smattering of it. As Father Pat described it, Latin was "the language of law and the language of God." Jeffrey planned on studying Latin in high school as soon as they let him.

He spotted his friends in church before the service began: Pablo with his parents and his sister, Maria; Marisol with her mother and Victor. And then he spotted Susie Norris. Like all the women in attendance, she wore a white veil over her head. Strands of brown hair curled up underneath it. She had the same inquisitive face as Jeffrey and she wore the same black glasses. She turned his way and saw him watching her. Jeffrey ducked his head. Had she seen him? If she thought he was checking her out, he would die of embarrassment. Maybe she just looked in his direction, but didn't actually see him.

He lifted his head slightly and stole a glance her way. She was staring directly at him. He ducked his head again. Now he really felt stupid. He felt a burn rising in his cheeks and knew he was blushing. He wanted to run right out of church, but Father Pat entered from the sacristy and Mass began.

After Mass, he slipped out a side door and hurried down the sidewalk. He thought he had gotten away clean and was startled when Susie stepped out from behind a bush and appeared directly in front of him.

"Where do you think you're going, mister?" she said. Susie was as pugnacious as a bulldog when she wanted to be, and she often wanted to be. "You don't even say hi to me at church?" Her veil was gone and she blinked at him behind her glasses.

"I didn't see you," Jeffrey said, cringing inside. How could he lie after he'd just gone to Mass?

"I saw you looking at me!"

"I wasn't sure that was you," he lied again. "You had that veil over your head."

"Yeah, right. Tell me about this car you're looking for."

"Car? What car?" Was that a lie? He wasn't sure.

"Don't play dumb with me," Susie insisted. "I talked to Marisol and she said you're looking for an old gray Porsche."

"Oh, that car. That's old news. I'm not looking for it anymore." More lies. If she didn't stop badgering him, he was going straight to hell.

"I know you've got a mystery on your hands, buster, and I want in. Don't forget, I'm the one who helped you solve your last case."

"You didn't solve that case," Jeffrey said, his voice rising. "That was Pablo and me!"

"Yeah, but it was my inspiration that helped. Without me, Marisol's poor brother would still be in jail."

"That's not true!" Jeffrey practically shouted.

"It is true. And don't forget, I have a cell phone." Susie slid her phone out of her jacket pocket and brandished it like the Hope Diamond. "I'm the one who called the police when the trouble started, remember?"

Jeffrey stared at the girl, his nostrils flaring. She was right about her phone. Jeffrey had a phone in his basement bedroom, but his parents wouldn't let him have a cell phone. Neither would Pablo's parents, or Marisol's mother. If the meeting with Charlie was a trap, then a phone might come in handy.

"Well, make up your mind," Susie demanded. "Am I in or not?"

"Meet us after school tomorrow," was all Jeffrey said. He stepped past her and continued down the sidewalk.

"I knew you'd see it my way," Susie called after him. "My way is always the right way!"

Jeffrey cringed.

That night, he sat at his mother's computer and checked

emails. One email in particular caught his eye: *Hi Jeffrey, I'm just making sure that you're coming tomorrow. Charlie.*

Yes, I'm coming, Jeffrey typed. Then he stared at the computer screen. There was something mysterious, something not quite right about this stranger they were going to meet. He couldn't put his finger on it, but years of solving mysteries had given him almost a sixth sense, a heightened intuition alerting him to hazards. He thought and he thought, but the answer wouldn't come. Perhaps he would have his answer tomorrow.

Chapter 10

It was hard for Jeffrey and his friends to get through Monday. The suspense of meeting Charlie and possibly finding the gray Porsche that hit Mr. Beasley kept them watching the clock all day long. To make matters worse, once school was out, Jeffrey and Susie had to wait for Marisol to finish cheer practice, and for Pablo to finish football practice. It was almost too much to bear, but by late afternoon they were all seated together in the back of a bus and headed to Sun Valley.

"Where are we meeting this Charlie?" Susie asked.

"He gave me an address by a strip mall," Jeffrey said. "I just hope we can find it before it gets dark."

"Is Charlie cute?"

Jeffrey turned to her with an angry look on his face. "What?"

"This Charlie guy, is he cute?"

Pablo and Marisol laughed.

"How would I know?" Jeffrey exploded. "This is an investigation, not a high school dance!"

Heads of other bus passengers turned and looked their way.

"Can't investigations be fun?" Susie asked.

"Not my investigations."

"Oh, so it's your investigation now. Well, excuse me." Susie crossed her arms over her chest and stared out the bus window. She stewed in silence for a few seconds, and then turned quietly to Marisol and whispered, "Marisol, is Charlie cute?"

Jeffrey spun around in his bus seat. "That does it! You're off the case!"

"You can't do that!"

"I just did!"

"Fine! I'm off the case and I'll take my phone with me. If you get in any trouble, tough luck. Not you, Pablo and Marisol, *him!*" She tilted her chin in Jeffrey's direction.

"Good!" Jeffrey said. "Get off at the next stop."

Susie sat straight up. "Don't you dare tell me what to do! You can kick me off your stupid investigation, but I'm still on the same bus as you, and I'm going in the same direction as you, so I think I'll just tag along as an impartial observer. How do you like them apples?" She folded her arms defiantly across her chest and stuck out her lower lip in a pout.

Pablo and Marisol howled with laughter.

Jeffrey simmered and stared out the window. His neck was hot and his temper hotter. Why, oh why, did he ever let Susie Norris come along?

The sun was fading and casting long shadows when they clamored off the bus in Sun Valley. They trudged to the designated street corner where Charlie had emailed Jeffrey to meet. Under a street light, they waited.

Behind them was a tattoo parlor; in front of them, a bar; a pawn shop and a bail bonds office completed the picture. Angry shouts came from the bail bonds office and shadows played across its windows. A pit bull, tied to a post not far from them, snarled and snapped in their direction. Rock music pounded from the bar with a pulsating bass that rattled their bones.

"Great place for a meeting, Jeffrey," Susie shouted above the din. "Just great. I feel real safe here."

"You're an impartial observer," Jeffrey reminded her. "Be quiet and observe."

"I observe us all getting robbed."

Jeffrey sighed and checked his watch.

The front door to the bar banged open. A blast of music and a man in tattered clothes spilled out. He stumbled past them, reeking of stale beer and cigarettes, and weaved his way down the sidewalk.

Marisol winced. Pablo pulled his shirt up over his nose to mitigate the stench.

"Like I said," Susie called out loudly.

"This is where Charlie told us to meet," Jeffrey called back, "so this is where we'll wait. He should be here any minute."

"I'm just glad *Pablo* is here. If anything happens, *he* can protect us."

Jeffrey stiffened. He started to respond, thought better of it, and closed his mouth.

Marisol gave Pablo a playful punch on the arm. He looked at her and smiled.

Ten minutes passed. Then another ten minutes.

A mud splattered car with tinted windows prowled past them. Gravel crunched and popped underneath its tires. The driver's window oozed down to reveal a greasy man with a mustache and dark glasses behind the wheel. He looked the girls over and whistled wolfishly.

Marisol nudged closer to Pablo. Susie reached for her cell phone. The driver laughed scornfully and stomped on the gas. The engine roared, tires spun, and the car raced off, spraying gravel. Jeffrey and his friends covered their eyes and faces, coughing and waving away the dust.

More minutes passed. It was dark now. Adults passed them on their way to the bar, giving them strange looks.

"This is ridiculous," Susie said.

"We'll give him five more minutes," Jeffrey said.

The five minutes passed and Jeffrey sighed. As they turned to leave, an angular body, hunched forward and hidden inside a hoodie, emerged from the shadows of an alley. They stopped and watched as the figure came running and pulled up two feet in front of them.

"Jeffrey?" the figure asked.

"Yes?"

"I'm Charlie." The hood came down and standing before them was a girl.

Chapter 11

"You're Charlie?" Jeffrey sputtered. He stared at the girl in front of him. She was his age, but taller, with blond hair pulled back in a ponytail, green eyes that seemed to glow in the dark, and a dash of freckles plastered across the bridge of her nose.

"Actually, my name's Charlotte, like *Charlotte's Web,* but my friends call me Charli, with an 'i' at the end. When I emailed you I spelled my name with an 'e' at the end, so you'd think I was a guy."

"But why did you do that?" Jeffrey asked.

"Because most guys think girls don't know anything about cars," Charlotte explained. "I wasn't sure if you'd take me seriously if you knew I was a girl, and I really need that fifty bucks."

Susie laughed out loud. "Looks like the joke's on you, Jeffrey Jones."

"I know it was a lie," Charlotte confessed, "and I'm sorry, but I think I found the gray Porsche you're looking for. If you want to talk it over with your friends, I understand. I'll wait in the alley." She flipped the hood up over her head and trotted back into the shadows.

Jeffrey turned to his friends. "What do you think?"

"We've come this far, we might as well go look at the car,"

Pablo said.

"What do you say, Marisol?"

"I like her. I think we should go."

Jeffrey turned to Susie. "And you?"

"And me what? I'm just an observer, my opinion doesn't count."

Jeffrey thought for a moment, and then followed Charlotte into the alley. He found her leaning against a brick wall, her face hidden in shadows. "Okay," he said, "let's see the car."

Chapter 12

Tramping their way across a barren, trash-littered field in the dead of night was not at all what Jeffrey and his friends had planned on. Yet here they were, seemingly cut off from civilization, where no one could hear them if they screamed.

The bone-rattling music of the bar had long since faded, replaced by a chorus of crickets and the incessant buzz of mosquitoes, who made their presence felt with little pin-prick bites on the arm and neck.

"Why are we going this way?" Susie asked, with an irritated tinge to her voice. She trailed behind the others and slapped at a mosquito that landed on her neck.

"I don't want anyone to see us," Charlotte answered, calling over her shoulder. She led the group with Jeffrey walking alongside of her. "The man who owns the car is scary."

"Scary how?" Pablo asked. He and Marisol trudged alongside of each other, a few yards behind Jeffrey and Charlotte.

"Scary-scary," Charlotte replied. "He's big and he's mean and he talks like zis." She spoke with a guttural voice, imitating a man's foreign accent.

"Is he German?" Marisol asked. She was fluent in English and Spanish, and she was studying German in school.

"I guess so," Charlotte responded. She glanced over her shoulder at Marisol.

"There are bugs here!" Susie called from the rear. She slapped at another mosquito.

"Sorry," Charlotte called back. She glanced at Jeffrey as he walked next to her and spoke to him quietly. "By the way, I've heard about you."

"You've heard about *me?*" Jeffrey asked, surprised.

"Aren't you the kid who caught those art thieves and got that guy out of jail?"

"That was me and Pablo," Jeffrey said. "And Marisol and Susie helped."

Charlotte nodded. "I've heard about you."

Jeffrey was stunned. Who was this strange girl? He felt an odd sort of curiosity about her and suddenly felt quite confused.

"We have school tomorrow," Susie called out, reminding them all.

"We're almost there," Charlotte called back. She leaned in close to Jeffrey and whispered, "Who is that girl?"

"That's Susie Norris."

"She's a little annoying, isn't she?"

Jeffrey laughed.

"What's so funny?" Susie said.

"Shhh!" Charlotte suddenly cautioned. "Everybody, Shhh!"

Ahead of them, at the end of the field, lay a single dilapidated house. The moon hung in the sky behind it, silhouetting the house like an eerie specter.

"That's the house!" Charlotte whispered.

She lowered her body and ran in a crouch towards a small hill. The others stooped down and followed her, circling their way up the hill.

Charlotte slid down on her belly on the hilltop and the others fanned out around her. The house was below them. A single car sat parked in the driveway, illuminated by an exposed bulb above the garage. It was an old gray Porsche with a dented front end.

"Is that the car?" Marisol whispered.

"Sure looks like it, huh, Jeffrey?" said Pablo.

"We'll have to get a closer look," Jeffrey said. "Susie, can you take a picture with your phone?"

"I'm just an observer, remember?"

"Oh, come on! Don't start with that, we need a picture!"

"Alright, but you owe me, mister. Big time."

The five sleuths crept quietly over the hill and approached the car. The air was so still, they could hear themselves breathe.

"Susie, get a picture from the front, showing the damage," Jeffrey whispered. "And get the license plate number."

Susie took out her cell phone and snapped away. "Got 'em."

"Do I get the reward money?" Charlotte asked.

"We'll have to report what we found to the police," Jeffrey told her. "But if this turns out to be the car, and it looks like it could be, you'll get the money. In the meantime, let's get out of here!"

He turned to run, the others behind him, but they all stopped in their tracks. Blocking their path at the end of the driveway was an enormous fat man. His face looked strained and furious, and he held a gun in his hand, pointed directly at them.

Chapter 13

Neither Jeffrey nor any of his friends had ever stared down the cold barrel of a gun. They stood frozen; eyes wide open, wondering if this moment and the man standing before them were really occurring, or if it was all just a horrible dream.

The man's face was fleshy, with beads of glistening sweat on his forehead and upper lip. Menace seemed to ooze from his every pore, as hot and sticky as the night air. His eyes narrowed behind his thick-lensed spectacles as he looked them over. For a long moment, he said nothing, then he curled his lip into a sneer and hissed, "You come to steal the treasure."

Summoning the courage to speak, Jeffrey said, "No, sir. We were just leaving." He took a step as if to leave, but the man shouted, "Nein!"

Jeffrey froze.

The man waved his gun. "Hands up."

Jeffrey and his friends raised their hands.

The man waved his gun towards the open garage. "Inside."

It was a dusty old garage with an ancient filing cabinet, a desk, and a metal cart that was covered with rusty tools and an assortment of lead pipes. Jeffrey and his friends stepped inside, hands held high. The fat man followed them in, turned on the light, and slammed the garage door down behind them. He stepped towards the cart and waved his gun at the concrete floor. "Down!"

The five sleuths dropped instantly to the floor, their hearts pounding. The man said nothing. With an icy stare, he looked them over, one by one. Finally, his gaze settled on Pablo.

"You," he said. "You with muscles. Stand up."

Pablo glanced at Jeffrey, and then rose shakily to his feet.

Still holding the gun, the man opened a drawer of the filing cabinet. He pulled out a tangle of thick rope and hurled it at Pablo. "Tie them. Hands behind back."

As Pablo untangled the mass of rope, Susie cleared her throat and spoke with a trembling voice, "I hope you know this is kidnapping."

"Shut up." The fat man turned to Pablo and gestured at Marisol with his gun. "Start with the pretty one."

Pablo sighed, took a length of rope, and stepped behind Marisol. The man looked her over with a malicious grin. "Don't cry, pretty one."

"I'm not scared of you," Marisol said, putting her hands behind her back.

"You will be." He gestured at Pablo with his gun. "Hurry."

Pablo looped a length of rope over Marisol's wrists and tied a knot. "Sorry, Marisol," he whispered.

"Shut up!" the man commanded.

"If we scream, somebody might hear us," Charlotte said.

The man sneered. "If you scream, I shoot."

Pablo finished with Marisol and stepped behind Susie. She put her hands behind her back. Pablo tied her wrists and moved on to Charlotte.

Jeffrey, who had been observing the man carefully, spoke up, trying his best to sound unafraid. "Sir, it's obvious you've mistaken us for someone else. We don't know anything about a treasure."

"Silence!" The man looked ready to explode. "You came here to steal the treasure!"

"And if we did," Jeffrey said calmly, "I suppose you think we could just steal your treasure like magic?" As he said the word 'magic,' Jeffrey shot a quick glance at Pablo. It was a tiny movement, almost imperceptible, but just enough for Pablo to catch. And Pablo knew exactly what Jeffrey was telling him.

When the boys were in the fifth grade, they had been fascinated with the legendary magician and escape artist Harry Houdini. From studying Houdini's life, they'd learned that one of his escape techniques was to quietly inhale and expand his muscles while being tied up. Later, by exhaling and relaxing his body he created just enough slack to wriggle out of his binds. It was a technique that the boys had practiced and used successfully in some magic shows they'd put on at school.

"Ah-ha!" the man exclaimed, seizing on Jeffrey's words. "You did come for the treasure!"

"Maybe we did and maybe we didn't," Jeffrey said.

The girls looked at him, confused and frightened. Why was he letting the man think they knew about his treasure?

"Enough with games, you tell me now," the man demanded.

"I'll tell you," Jeffrey said. "But first you have to let the others go."

The man slammed his fist down on the metal cart. Pipes and tools bounced in the air and landed in jangles. "You think I am stupid?"

"No, sir," Jeffrey said. "You seem like a very smart man. Smart enough to take advantage of the opportunity I'm offering."

"And what opportunity is this?"

"The opportunity to protect your treasure."

The fat man laughed. "Now you are the stupid one. You think the treasure is here?" He laughed harder. Turning to Pablo, he gestured at Jeffrey with his gun. "Tie the fat boy up."

"I'm not fat, I'm barrel-chested," Jeffrey said, shooting another look at Pablo.

The man roared with laughter. "You are fat and funny!" To Pablo: "Tie him."

Pablo stepped behind Jeffrey and looped a length of rope around his chest. He noticed that Jeffrey had clenched his fists tight and was inhaling quietly, expanding his ribcage and flexing his arm muscles. Jeffrey spoke to the man while Pablo tied him. "If the treasure's not here, where is it?"

"That is what you are going to tell me."

Pablo finished tying Jeffrey and looked at the man. "We don't know anything about a treasure, mister."

The man stared hard at Jeffrey, his eyes narrowing. "He does. Now bring me the rope and turn around."

Pablo handed the man what was left of the rope, turned around, and put his hands behind his back. The man laid his gun on the metal cart. Smiling, he hooked the rope around Pablo's wrists and yanked it hard. Pablo winced as the rope bit into his skin. The man tied a tight knot and shoved Pablo forward. The boy stumbled and fell, hitting the concrete floor with a thud.

"Stop it!" Marisol cried.

The fat man laughed.

"Looks like I was wrong," Jeffrey said. "You're not a smart man, are you?"

"Jeffrey, don't!" Marisol pleaded.

"And you are a bold fat boy," the man said. He stepped forward and slapped Jeffrey hard across the face, jostling his glasses. A race of blood flushed Jeffrey's cheek.

The girls screamed.

"Now you tell me what you know," the man said.

Jeffrey stifled his tears. "I'll be happy to tell you. But first you have to let the others go."

The man's face turned hard. He slapped Jeffrey again, harder this time. Jeffrey's glasses flew across the garage.

Marisol and Susie screamed.

"Stop hitting him," Pablo shouted.

"No more games," the man said tersely. He went to the cart and picked up a sheet of paper. He stared at the paper and read from it aloud: *"I'm wrong, but I could be right. Catch me twice if you can."* He lowered the paper and stared hard at Jeffrey.

Jeffrey blinked and squinted. Without his glasses, everything was a blur. "It sounds like a puzzle," he said.

"Of course, it's a puzzle! What does it mean?"

"Is there more to it, or is that all?"

The man looked at the paper and read: *"I am a hidden room. Approach my outer walls, find nothing. Look within. See kings plunder the headless ghost. One step beyond the grave."* He lifted his eyes from the paper and looked at Jeffrey.

"Well, the first part is easy," Jeffrey said.

"Tell me."

"I'll tell you. But you have to let the others go."

The man's face swelled red with anger.

"I'll stay with you, Jeffrey," Pablo said. "Let the girls go, mister."

"I'll stay, too," Marisol said.

"Guys, don't!" Susie shrieked. "Stop it!"

The fat man eyed Susie carefully. He set the paper back on the metal cart and picked up a blowtorch. "We start with you," he said. He lit the blowtorch, setting its blue flame hissing, and stepped forward.

"Jeffrey, do something!" Charlotte cried.

Jeffrey felt the heat from the blowtorch brush his face as the man stepped past him. Susie stiffened and closed her eyes. The man's grubby fingers took hold of her hair. She screamed.

"Stop!" Jeffrey shouted. "Stop, I'll tell you!"

The man paused and looked at Jeffrey, the flame from the blowtorch inches from Susie's hair.

"The first part," Jeffrey began, "the first part is a clock."

The man blinked. "A clock?"

"Yes, don't you see? A broken clock tells the wrong time, but it can be right twice a day. And people can chase time, but they can never catch it. Get it?"

Excitement flickered over the man's face. He turned the blowtorch off and hurried back to the metal cart. Grabbing the paper, he read from it again: "*I am a hidden room. Approach my outer walls, find nothing. Look within. See kings plunder the headless ghost. One step beyond the grave.*" He looked at Jeffrey.

"That part is harder," Jeffrey said. "I need more time."

"You tell me now," the man insisted.

"I can't tell you now, because I don't know."

The man lifted the blowtorch and lit the flame.

"Don't!" Susie cried.

"Jeffrey, don't let him do it!" Charlotte said.

A cell phone rang. The man turned off the blowtorch, reached in his pocket and extracted a phone. He answered in German.

Jeffrey watched the man carefully. Speaking gruffly into his phone, the man set the blowtorch on the cart. He stepped into the house, closing the door behind him, and leaving them alone in the garage.

"What do we do now?" Charlotte cried, but Jeffrey never heard her. The moment the man stepped out of the garage, Jeffrey blew all the air out of his lungs and relaxed his chest and arms, loosening his binds ever so slightly. He worked his hands and wrists feverishly through the slack in the rope, twisting and squirming like a contortionist. The man's voice could be heard, speaking in German, from the house. "Marisol," Jeffrey whispered, "Listen to his conversation. Try to remember everything he says."

Marisol nodded and listened. "He says he has four kids that he thinks are spies and he's going to make them talk."

Susie and Charlotte gasped.

"Stay calm," Pablo told them. He watched as Jeffrey

continued to squirm his way through the ever-loosening rope, a tiny fraction at a time. The two boys had practiced rope escapes many times when they were younger. If only Jeffrey could do it again now. "Come on, Houdini," Pablo urged.

"I'm almost out," Jeffrey said, and in a moment, he was, shedding the rope and pulling his arms free.

The girls shrieked. Jeffrey scrambled across the concrete floor, grabbed his glasses and put them on. Able to see now, he ran to Pablo and set to work untying him.

"Hurry, Jeffrey," Marisol whispered breathlessly. "He says he's going to use the blowtorch to make us talk!"

Though he was not known to panic, Jeffrey was close. The rope around Pablo's wrists was heavy and coarse and tied in knots that seemed impossibly tight. Sweat trickled from his forehead and seeped from every pore in his body. His shirt was drenched and his hands trembled as he tried in vain to untie his friend.

"Hurry, Jeffrey," Susie pleaded.

"Look on the cart," Pablo suggested. "Maybe there's a knife."

Jeffrey sprang to his feet and ran to the metal cart.

"Faster, Jeffrey!" Charlotte cried.

Rummaging through pipes and tools, Jeffrey found a pair of scissors and ran back to Pablo's side. He began to cut and hack his way through the thick rope.

"Come on, Jeffrey!" Pablo whispered.

"I'm getting it!" Jeffrey said excitedly. Seconds later, Pablo was free.

The girls gave a sound of elation. Pablo turned to Marisol and worked on her binds. Jeffrey did the same to Charlotte.

"What am I, chopped liver?" Susie said.

"Shhh!" Jeffrey said, "We'll get to you."

He finished untying Charlotte and started on Susie. "It's about time," she said.

"Shhh!"

"Guys, he's coming back!" Charlotte said.

They heard footsteps from the house and everyone froze.

Jeffrey took off his glasses and slipped them into his shirt pocket. "Pretend like you're still tied up."

They took their positions back on the floor with their hands behind their backs. The footsteps from the house grew closer. Pablo suddenly jumped up and ran to the metal cart. He grabbed a pipe and leapt back, joining the others on the floor, and holding the pipe hidden behind his back.

The door to the house opened and the fat man stepped back into the garage, eyeing them carefully.

"You better let us go," Charlotte said.

He ignored her and picked up the blowtorch. "We start again. You tell me about the treasure." He eyed Marisol and a sinister smile crept over his face. "It's your turn, pretty one." He lit the blowtorch, its flame hissing in the airless garage.

Marisol's eyes grew wide. Jeffrey glanced at her, and then at Pablo. The fat man stepped out from behind the cart. Pablo gripped the pipe tightly behind his back. The man stepped past him, and then Pablo struck. The pipe caught the back of the man's leg with a sharp crack. The leg crumpled and the man hit the floor with a heavy grunt.

"Run!" Pablo shouted.

Five bodies leapt to their feet. Jeffrey swung the garage door open. Pablo gave the groaning man another crack on the leg with the pipe. They all ran out the garage door and into the night.

Chapter 14

Hearts pounding against their chests, they ran as fast as they could across the desolate, moonlit field, and they didn't dare look back. All they could think about was putting as much ground between themselves and the blowtorch-wielding fat man as they possibly could. All they could hear was their breath, coming in heavy pants, and their shoes slapping against the barren earth.

Hearing the music from the bar, which before had seemed so distasteful, was now a relief. They reached the street light where they'd first met Charlotte and pulled up.

"Susie, call the police," Marisol gasped between heavy breaths.

"I'm on it!"

Jeffrey pulled out a pen and scribbled furiously on a scrap of paper. Susie gaped at him. "What are you doing?"

"Writing down those treasure clues before I forget."

"Are you crazy? We could have been killed!"

"There's still a treasure out there."

"How can you think about a treasure at a time like this?"

"Actually, I'm pretty excited," Jeffrey said. "A valuable treasure, a sinister fat man ... what more could you want?"

"Now I know you're crazy!"

"You can keep your sinister fat man," Pablo said. "I'm just

glad we're alive."

"Me, too," said Marisol.

"Me, three," said Susie.

"Hey, wait a minute," Pablo said. "Where's Charlotte?"

The four of them stopped, looked at each other, and then glanced around in the darkness. Charlotte was nowhere to be found. The girl had completely disappeared.

Jeffrey's father slammed his fist down on the kitchen table with a resounding crack. "How stupid can you be?"

Jeffrey didn't reply. His father sat across from him at the table, and his mother stood with her back against the stove and her arms folded across her chest. It was well past midnight and Jeffrey had school in the morning, but both he and his parents were wide awake.

"I didn't know it was going to turn out the way it did," Jeffrey said quietly.

"You didn't know?" his father asked in mock astonishment. "Did you hear that Evelyn? He didn't know. 'Gee, Mom; gee, Dad; I didn't know it would be dangerous to sneak off to Sun Valley in the middle of the night and spy on a strange man.' Of all the stupid excuses I've heard over the years, this one takes the cake, boy."

Jeffrey withdrew deeper into himself and shrunk into his chair. He felt six inches tall.

Mr. Jones pushed off from the table and paced the room. "You know, Jeffrey, when you and Pablo built those motorized go-carts, and went racing up and down the street, terrorizing all the neighbors, I didn't get mad. When that monkey escaped from the zoo and you guys found him and hid him in the basement for three days, feeding him bananas and teaching him how to dance, I didn't get mad. But this time, boy, I'm mad. I'm steaming mad."

"What were you thinking, Jeffrey?" his mother asked softly.

"He wasn't thinking!" shouted Mr. Jones. "That's the whole point! I hear from his teachers, 'Oh, Jeffrey this! Oh, Jeffrey that! Why, he's the smartest boy in school!' What a crock!" He turned to Jeffrey. "Do you realize you could have been killed pulling a stunt like this?"

Jeffrey stared at the table.

"Well, do you?"

"I guess so."

"You guess so?" Mr. Jones threw up his hands and turned to his wife. "The boy genius guesses so." He turned back to Jeffrey. "The police said when they got to that house in Sun Valley, it was deserted. That means that madman with the blowtorch is still on the loose. He could be looking for you right now."

"Jeffrey," said his mother, "do you have any idea how frightened we were when the police called here and told us what happened?"

"I'm sorry, Mom. I thought I was helping Mr. Beasley, my teacher."

"Your teacher?" Mr. Jones was aghast. "Where does your teacher get off hiring two kids to play detective for him? You wait till I get through with that Schmeasley!"

"His name is Beasley," Jeffrey said, "and you don't have to yell at him. It's not his fault."

"You bet it's his fault! I'll see that he never teaches again! As for you, you're grounded until further notice. And you better plan on that being a long time. Like the rest of your life."

Jeffrey's face drained of color. He pushed off from the kitchen table and rose shakily to his feet.

"Where are you going?" his father asked.

"To my room."

"I want you to think about what you did," his father said, "and how horrified your mother and I were to get a call from the police telling us you were kidnapped."

"I will. I'm sorry." Jeffrey turned to his mother. "I'm sorry, Mom."

"I know, Jeffrey."

Jeffrey bowed his head and walked out. Descending the stairs to his room in the basement, he heard his father's voice: "Unbelievable. Simply unbelievable. I can't believe I raised a son to be that stupid."

Jeffrey winced. Of all the things his father had said, that was the most hurtful. He reached the bottom of the stairs and turned on the light. His room looked cramped and cluttered, something he'd never noticed before. This room looks as small as I feel, he thought to himself.

He changed into his bed clothes, said his nightly prayers, and turned out the light. As he crawled into bed and stared up at the ceiling, his eyes adjusted slowly to the darkness.

He heard his parents talking loudly upstairs, and then their voices quieted, and the shaft of light that began in the kitchen and shone down the basement stairs went off. He followed the sound of his parents' footsteps from the kitchen to their bedroom and soon the house was quiet. He was alone now and able to think.

He wondered if his parents would have felt sorry for him and not yelled so much if the fat man had burned him with the blowtorch. He knew it was a stupid thought, and he banished it from his mind just as quickly as it had sprung up.

Still, it hurt that his parents never seemed to appreciate him. He knew he was smart, his teachers knew he was smart; how come his parents never acknowledged that he was smart? And why were they always so overprotective of him, always treating him like he was a kid? Was it going to be this way the rest of his life?

He thought about the treasure and the clues the fat man had given them. Maybe if he could solve the puzzle and find the treasure, maybe then his parents would appreciate him.

He yawned. The long day's events caught up with him and suddenly he felt very tired. The softness of his bed, the physical surrender of his body, his eyelids felt heavy and he closed them. Sleep was seconds away when he abruptly shot up in bed. *Charlotte!*

She disappeared when they escaped from the fat man, but she was the one who had led them all there. Maybe she had tried contacting him. He listened carefully, and when he was sure his parents were asleep, he slipped quietly out of bed and crept up the basement stairs.

Picking his way carefully around floorboards that creaked, he made his way to the living room. The room was dark and silent, save for the eerie glow of the aquarium lights and the bubbling water of the tank. Jeffrey slid into the chair at his mother's desk and turned on the computer. He checked his emails and saw one marked urgent and sent from Charlotte. He opened the email and stared at it:

I have to talk to you! You and your friends are all in great danger!

Chapter 15

"I've never been grounded before in my life! Ever!"

Susie spoke in a harsh whisper, spittle flying. She sat across the aisle from Jeffrey in the back of history class, and leaned towards him. "Now, thanks to you, Jeffrey Jones, that's all over! I've lost everything! My permanent record is ruined!"

Jeffrey simmered. He kept his eyes on their teacher, Mrs. Daniels, at the front of the classroom, and when she turned around to write on the blackboard, he whispered back to Susie. "I tried my best to keep you away from the case, but you and your big mouth wouldn't get off the bus. You've got no one to blame but yourself!"

"*My* big mouth? Look who's talking! You think you're so smart, well I've got news for you, you're nothing but a –" She leaned in close and whispered in Jeffrey's ear. Jeffrey's eyes snapped wide open.

"Susie Norris!" The words sliced like a knife across the quiet of the classroom. Mrs. Daniels stood at the front of the room, her hands on her hips.

Jeffrey sat straight up in his seat. Susie shrank deeper into hers. Mrs. Daniels stood staring at them both. "That's quite a conversation you and Jeffrey are having in my classroom. Perhaps you'd like to share it with the rest of us."

Heads turned. Jeffrey and Susie felt the eyes of their classmates upon them.

"That's not a good idea," Susie muttered.

"Why, it's an excellent idea," countered Mrs. Daniels. "Please tell us what you just whispered in Jeffrey's ear?"

The class leaned forward, eager to hear. Susie squirmed nervously in her seat. Jeffrey sat perfectly still, his eyes locked on the teacher. "Well?" said Mrs. Daniels.

"I'd rather not," Susie said.

"Oh, but I insist. We're all eager to hear."

"Very well." Susie sat up straight and cleared her throat. "I called Jeffrey Jones a pompous ass."

The class exploded in laughter. Mrs. Daniels stood open-mouthed and speechless. Jeffrey sat rigid, his face aflame. He wished the floor would open up and swallow him whole and he could disappear from the world forever.

The lunchtime cafeteria at Trinity High was a scene of organized chaos. Freshmen and sophomores composed the early lunch period, and they were herded in, hustled through an assembly line of servers and kitchen workers, and then turned loose on the cafeteria floor.

In a quick twenty minutes, they would be rushed out of the cafeteria and back into their classrooms, in order to make room for the juniors and seniors, but for now they held center stage. There were hundreds of them, engaged in lively chatter, laughter, and the occasional scream.

A smattering of strategically placed teachers stood watch, casting a wary eye, while their own stomachs grumbled. That today's special was veal cutlets, green beans, and mashed potatoes only increased their impatience. The smell permeated the air and led to a constant checking of watches as they counted the minutes until they could escape to the teacher's lounge for their own lunch period.

In the eye of the storm, surrounded by tables of chattering freshmen, Jeffrey sat with his friends, Pablo and Marisol. They leaned in close over their table and spoke in hushed tones. Jeffrey told them about Charlotte's email.

"We're in danger?" Pablo said. "What kind of danger?"

"I don't know," Jeffrey replied. "But I'll find out. I'm meeting Charlotte after school. I wish you guys could come, but I know you have football and cheer practice."

"What about Susie?" Marisol asked.

Jeffrey leaned back in his chair and waved his arm disgustedly. "Susie's mad. She's never been grounded before."

"Me, neither," said Marisol, "but my mom gave me a week."

"I got six days," said Pablo.

"I got life," said Jeffrey.

"*Life?*" Marisol exclaimed. She'd never heard of anyone

being grounded for life before.

Jeffrey stared down at the table. Even when his parents weren't there, they still made him feel small. "That's what my dad said."

"So we're still on the case?" Pablo asked.

"Absolutely, we're still on the case. Did your dad say anything about us dropping the case?"

Pablo furrowed his brow. "Not really. I mean, he yelled a lot, but he never said anything specifically about dropping the case."

"My dad did the same thing. He yelled so much he forgot about that. So technically, we're okay. At least, I think so. Marisol?"

Marisol shook her head. "My mom yelled a lot, but she never mentioned the case. She doesn't even know there is a case."

"Well, there you go."

Pablo took a swig of milk from his half-pint carton. Marisol turned to Jeffrey with a look of concern. "Are you really grounded for life, Jeffrey?"

Jeffrey shrugged. "I'm hoping for an early parole."

Pablo laughed and choked on his milk. It poured out his nose and almost out his ears.

Marisol screamed and jumped back from the table.

The cafeteria roared with laughter.

Chapter 16

Jeffrey was shocked when he saw Charlotte waiting for him on the sidewalk in front of school. The night before, she'd been half-hidden in the shadows and underneath her hoodie. Standing before him now, in the light of day, she looked much prettier.

She wore a sleeveless summer dress and her blond hair was down and loose around her shoulders. The sun bounced off her freckles and gave her hair a golden sheen, and when she smiled, as she did when she saw Jeffrey approaching, her entire face lit up.

"I'm sorry I left you guys," she said, "but I thought that man with the blowtorch was going to kill us all and I freaked out. I ran home as fast as I could."

"I understand," Jeffrey said.

Kids from school walked past, giving them startled looks. Jeffrey knew they were wondering who Charlotte was, and what someone like her was doing talking to someone like him. She was tall, slender, and beautiful. He was short, chunky, and looked like an owl. His insecurities only increased when Charlotte touched his arm.

"Listen," she said, "is there someplace where we can sit and talk?"

"Actually, I'm grounded," Jeffrey said. "So I only have a

few minutes. But we can talk as we walk. I live pretty close to here."

Charlotte nodded and they started off together down the sidewalk. She took a quick glance over her shoulder at Jeffrey's school. "So what do they teach you in Catholic school?"

"The same thing they teach you at your school," Jeffrey said, "only with religion and morality thrown in."

"Religion and morality," Charlotte snorted. "Do they make you go to church?"

"Yeah, but I go anyway." He gave her a quick look. "Do you?"

"*Me?*" Her tone implied that such an action was unthinkable. "If I walked into a church, I'd erupt in flames."

"Don't say that."

"It's true."

"God is very forgiving. Whatever you've done in the past, He'll forgive you. But you have to ask."

"I don't believe in God," she said softly.

"Why not?"

Charlotte stopped and looked at him as if it were the most ridiculous question in the world. "*Why not?*" Her eyes darted about as she searched for the right words to express herself. "Because if God is real, then why does He let so much bad stuff happen? Like wars and people killing each other?"

"People do those things, not God," Jeffrey said. "And the

people responsible for wars and killing are people who have rejected God or stopped believing in Him."

Charlotte laughed out loud. "Are you serious?"

"I'm very serious," Jeffrey told her. Then he repeated a pearl of wisdom that he'd learned from Father Pat: "Atheist communists killed more people in the 20th century than in all the wars fought in the entire history of the world combined. When they stopped believing in God, murder meant nothing to them."

"That's crazy! People don't need to believe in God to be good. And not everyone who believes in God is a good person."

Jeffrey faced her confidently. He was on solid ground now, engaged in a debate of ideas and intellect. "People who believe in God behave better than people who don't. Just like people who believe in traffic cops drive better than people who don't."

"You really believe that?"

"Of course, I believe it. It's the only logical answer. And I know a thing or two about logic."

"My mom's dead, Jeffrey," Charlotte said. "She believed in God, but she got cancer and died, and she was only thirty-seven years old. I was with her while she suffered. She withered away and looked like a skeleton when she died. If God is real, why did He do that to her?"

"I'm sorry about your mother," Jeffrey said. "I don't know

how to answer that. God works in mysterious ways."

"I didn't come here to talk about God," Charlotte snapped, her green eyes blazing. "I came here to tell you that you and your friends are all in danger."

"What kind of danger?"

Jeffrey didn't see the black sedan that raced up to the curb beside him and screeched to a stop. He spun around and the car's passenger door flew open. Sitting behind the wheel was a bull-necked man with a shaved head and a scruffy red goatee. The man's arm was draped over the top of the passenger seat and his windbreaker drawn back to reveal a 9 mm Glock 17 handgun resting in a holster, strapped across his side. Jeffrey saw the gun and his eyes widened.

"Get in the car," the man ordered.

Chapter 17

"Charlotte didn't tell you she had an uncle who was a cop?"

The man stared at Jeffrey with curious eyes, one hand on the steering wheel, the other hand pulling and twisting the red hair on his chin.

"No, sir," Jeffrey replied from the passenger seat.

"This is my Uncle Markus," Charlotte said, seated behind Jeffrey.

Markus pulled a wallet from the pocket of his windbreaker, flipped it open, and flashed a badge at Jeffrey's face. In a second, the wallet was back in his pocket. "You kids are lucky to be alive," he said. "That man with the blowtorch you tangled with is wanted in three countries and he's considered armed and dangerous."

"What's his name?" Jeffrey asked.

"I'll ask the questions," Markus snapped.

Jeffrey nodded and glanced sullenly around the car. It was a new sedan and it smelled of leather, cheap cologne, and stale cigarettes. Jeffrey noticed the car's ashtray was open and overflowing with crushed down cigarette butts. "I told the police everything I know," he said.

"And?"

"And that's it."

Markus sighed and shifted his position. The leather seat crinkled under his weight. "Charlotte tells me you're a smart kid."

Jeffrey glanced over his shoulder at Charlotte in the back seat. She smiled at him.

"Is she right?" Markus asked.

"I guess so."

"Well, if you guess so, tell me about this treasure the man was asking about."

"I don't know anything about a treasure," Jeffrey said. "I don't even know what kind of treasure it is."

Markus shot a look at Charlotte in the back seat. She shrugged.

"It's gold," Markus said. "Some trinkets, some diamonds maybe, but mostly gold." He paused for a moment to let his words sink in. "How's your history, kid? Hernan Cortez? The Spanish Conquistadors?"

Jeffrey nodded. "I've read about them."

"The Spanish hauled a lot of gold out of Mexico, but not all of it made its way back to Europe. Shipwrecks, pirates, human greed ... That's the kicker: greed. This gold we're talking about came from the Aztec Indians. It was meant for the Spanish Crown, but that's not where it ended up."

Jeffrey sat riveted as Markus spun his tale: "Twenty years ago, a German treasure hunter discovered the wreck of a Spanish galleon off the coast of France. The ship was loaded with gold. The treasure hunter was German, so the German government claimed the gold was theirs. The French government said it was their gold, since the ship was found off their coast. Because the gold originally came from Mexico, the Mexican government said it was theirs."

"What about the treasure hunter?" Jeffrey asked.

Markus let out a hearty laugh. "He said the gold was all his. The whole thing bogged down in a sea of lawsuits, until last year when the courts finally ruled in the treasure hunter's favor."

"So it's his treasure?" Jeffrey said

"Not quite. Do you know what's going on in Germany right now?"

"A little bit."

"Germany is under attack," Markus said, "by an army of so-called migrants. They're not migrants at all, they're an invading force. The country is being taken over. All of Europe is. Women are being assaulted. People are being run out of their homes. No one is safe."

"Can't the government do anything?" Jeffrey asked.

Markus laughed. "The government is behind it! The German Chancellor is a traitor to her country and her own people. The problem for her is the government's going broke. They're paying these invaders to occupy their own country and they've run out of money. So they've begun confiscating property from their own citizens. They're desperate and they have their sights set on that treasure. The treasure hunter got wind of what was happening and took matters into his own hands. He disappeared and took his treasure with him. No one has seen him since."

"Isn't this exciting, Jeffrey?" Charlotte said.

Jeffery turned to her and nodded.

"Tell Jeffrey about the letter, Uncle Markus."

Markus cleared his throat. "Two months ago, the treasure hunter's family received a letter from him, mailed from Los Angeles. Seems he was being followed and in fear for his life, so he hid the treasure and sent his family a clue to where it was hidden. One month later, his body was found here in North Hollywood. He was murdered."

"I suppose we should find the treasure and return it to his family," Jeffrey said.

"That'd be a neat trick," Markus said. "They're all dead."

"They were murdered, too, Jeffrey," Charlotte added.

Marcus fixed Jeffrey with a penetrating stare. "The treasure hunter's family was tied up and tortured with a blowtorch. Then shot in the head, execution style. The killer probably thought they knew where the treasure was hidden. They didn't and now they're dead. The killer is still on the loose and he's shown he'll stop at nothing to get his hands on that gold, including murder."

A cold shiver ran up Jeffrey's spine. "Was it the man we saw last night?"

Markus nodded grimly. "He wants that treasure. He wants it badly and he would have killed you kids to find it. You're lucky you escaped. We believe he's a mercenary, hired by the German government to bring them the treasure, by whatever means necessary. What I want to know is how much *you* know about where it could be hidden. The sooner we find it, the sooner we'll apprehend the man you encountered last night, and the more lives will be saved. Charlotte tells me you've already solved part of the puzzle."

"The man last night read us some clues," Jeffrey said. "Are those the same clues that the treasure hunter mailed to his family?"

Markus nodded.

"Well, in that case, the first part is a clock," Jeffrey said.

"What clock?"

"I don't know what clock, or where it is," Jeffrey told him. "I just know it's a clock."

"What about the rest of the clues?"

Jeffrey shook his head. "Everything from last night until today has been a blur. To be honest with you, I haven't had any time to study the other clues."

Markus pulled a crumpled sheet of paper from his pocket, unfolded it and read aloud: "*I am a hidden room. Approach my outer walls, find nothing. Look within. See kings plunder the headless ghost. One step beyond the grave.*" He lowered the paper and stared hard at Jeffrey. "What does that mean?"

Jeffrey shrugged.

Markus rattled the paper. "Don't play stupid with me, kid."

"I'm not. I honestly don't know."

"Charlotte said you were smart. She said you could help us solve this case and help save some lives."

"I'm sorry," Jeffrey said. "I'll go over the clues tonight. Maybe I can find something."

"Whatever you find, I want to know. Understand?"

Jeffrey nodded.

"Good. Whatever you come up with, tell Charlotte. She'll contact me. Any questions?"

Jeffrey shook his head. "No, I'll do what I can."

"All right. Get out of here."

Jeffrey opened the car door.

"One more thing," Markus said.

Jeffrey paused, one foot outside of the car, and one foot in, and looked over his shoulder at Markus.

"You try finding this treasure on your own," Markus said, "and I'll throw you in jail."

Chapter 18

"Answer me, Jeffrey."

His father's voice was harsh, but not without concern. "I asked you a question: Are we going to come home and find the house burned down?"

Jeffrey shifted uneasily in his seat. His parents sat across from him at the kitchen table. They'd just finished eating dinner and now he was avoiding his father's gaze. "No, Dad."

"No? Are you sure?" Mr. Jones turned to his wife. "What do you think, Evelyn? Can we trust this kid?"

Jeffrey's mother studied him for a long moment, and then pushed off from the table and went to the stove to tend to a pot of simmering coffee. "I think he'll be fine on his own for one day."

"Is your mother right, Jeffrey? I don't want a phone call from the police telling me you're in jail, or kidnapped, or dead."

"That won't happen," Jeffrey said.

"It better not, because we're going to be in San Diego for your mother's convention. You get in a scrape this time, and you're on your own."

Jeffrey's mother picked up the coffee pot with one hand and a coffee cup with the other. "Don't say that, Brad. Jeffrey, you know we're only a phone call away. We're leaving early Sunday morning and we'll be back before midnight. So we're only going to be gone for one day."

"I know, Mom."

Mr. Jones watched with expectant eyes as his wife returned to the kitchen table and poured him a steaming cup of coffee. "I can't wait till you have kids of your own, boy," he said to Jeffrey. "You'll see what it's like to get a midnight call from the police."

Jeffrey looked down at the table. He couldn't imagine himself married, much less having kids. Who'd want to marry him?

His father cradled the coffee cup in his hands and blew on the steam. Adopting his best Irish brogue, he said, "Hello, sir? Sergeant Peterson, Los Angeles Police Department. Do you have a son named Jeffrey? Well, guess what? He's been kidnapped. No worries, though. We found his body in a ditch."

"Brad! That's awful!" Mrs. Jones returned the coffee pot to the stove and took her seat back at the table.

Jeffrey squirmed. His parents were making him feel small again.

His father took a tentative sip of coffee and winced as the hot liquid burned his tongue. He set the cup back on the table. "I'll tell you what, kid. Your mother and I talked it over and we're putting an end to your grounding."

Jeffrey perked up. "Really?"

Mr. Jones held up his hand. "Now listen, this isn't a license to act like a fool. It's contingent on good behavior. You pull a stunt like this last one and all bets are off. You'll be grounded so fast it'll make your head spin."

"I know, I know! But can Pablo and Marisol come over?" He was already thinking of holding a meeting to go over the clues to the treasure.

"Hold on a second," his father said. "What did I just tell you? I don't want an army of kids running through the house while we're away."

"It's not an army of kids; it's just Pablo and Marisol, and maybe one other person." He'd meant Charlotte, but he realized immediately that he'd said too much. His parents were aware of Charlotte from the police report and the emails they'd exchanged. They'd never allow him to see her again.

His mother's eyebrows arched halfway up her forehead. "What other person?"

"Just someone I met," Jeffrey said, his body stiffening. His mother's instinct to know every detail of his life had been aroused. There was no going back now. The sleeping giant had awoken.

"Met where?"

"Around."

"Around where? And who is this person?" The pitch in his mother's voice was high and irritated. Jeffrey could feel her curiosity growing by the second.

"Just some kid," he said.

"What's the kid's name?" his father snapped, cutting through the clutter and pinning Jeffrey down.

Jeffrey held his breath. If his parents knew he was talking to Charlotte, they'd cancel their trip and sentence him to twenty years of solitary confinement in the basement. But he couldn't lie to his parents, could he? That was the worst sin imaginable. No, he just couldn't do that.

"Susie Norris," he said.

"Susie Norris?" His father nearly fell out of his chair. "You're hanging out with her?"

Mrs. Jones turned to her husband, indignation written over her face. "What's wrong with Susie Norris?"

"What's wrong with her?" Mr. Jones said. "She takes after her mother, that's what's wrong."

"And what does that mean?"

"It means she talks too much."

"That's a terrible thing to say!"

"It's true."

"I'm going to my room," Jeffrey said quietly. Neither parent heard him.

Mrs. Jones stared at her husband. "Doris Norris is one of my closest friends, and you're calling her a gossip?"

"I didn't say she was a gossip. I said she talks too much."

"Well, it's the same thing."

"No it's not."

Jeffrey rose silently from the table and slipped quietly out of the room.

"Next you'll be saying that I'm a gossip," he heard his mother say.

"Oh, come off it, Evelyn," his father replied.

"I will not come off it! You owe me an apology!"

"*What?*"

Jeffrey's parents were still arguing as he crept down the basement stairs. He felt awful about lying to them, but he knew that if he mentioned Charlotte's name, they'd call an end to his search for the treasure, and the fat man would continue killing people until he found it.

He said a quick prayer, asking God to forgive him for the lie he'd just told, and then he called Pablo on the basement phone and told him about his encounter with Charlotte's uncle Markus. When he hung up, he sat down at his desk with a copy of the treasure clues. He already knew the first part of the puzzle was a clock, but he had no idea what that meant or how it connected to the other clues.

He read the first three sentences of the second part: *I am a hidden room. Approach my outer walls, find nothing. Look within.*

That was simple enough, he thought. It told him that the key to the message lay buried within the words. Maybe it was in code. He had read books on cryptography – the art of breaking codes – but it could take days, maybe months to solve.

He read the next two sentences: *See kings plunder the headless ghost. One step beyond the grave.*

He didn't have a clue what those lines meant, but his mind zeroed in on the word *plunder*. It was an unusual word, a word usually associated with pirates. He reached for his dictionary, just to be sure. Yup, he was right. One of the definitions for "pirate" was to rob or plunder a ship.

Did the message have something to do with pirates? The missing gold had come from a sunken galleon, but it wasn't a pirate ship. Perhaps pirates had been the ones to sink the ship ...

He thought of famous pirates he had read or heard about: Long John Silver, Captain Kidd, Blackbeard ... could the message be referring to one of them? If so, why did it say, *See kings plunder*? Kings weren't the ones doing the plundering, although kings did send out naval vessels to combat pirates.

Jeffrey knew from reading that pirates were not the romantic adventurers portrayed in movies and on television. They were bloodthirsty killers and cutthroats, who were known to capture Christians and murder them or sell them into slavery. Thomas Jefferson, the third president of the United States, had to declare war on the pirates of the Barbary Coast in order to save American lives.

Among the many books spilling out of Jeffrey's bookcase,

were a couple on pirates. He reached for them, sat back at his desk, and spent the next two hours engrossed in tales of ships, pirates, and treasures of gold.

At ten o'clock, his mother called down from the top of the stairs: "Jeffrey, school tomorrow!"

"Okay, Mom," he called back, but going to bed was the furthest thing from his mind.

He said his nightly prayers, turned off the lights, and crawled into bed with his books and a flashlight. By midnight, he'd discovered an amazing fact: when the vicious pirate Blackbeard was finally killed by Lieutenant Robert Maynard, his head was cut off and hung from the ship's bowsprit, and his body was thrown overboard.

According to legend, when the pirate's body hit the water, the head hanging from the bowsprit shouted, "Come on, Edward!" and the headless body swam three times around the ship before sinking to the bottom. Ever since that day, the legend continued, Blackbeard's ghost has searched for his missing head.

As Jeffrey read those words, a chill swept over his body. Was Blackbeard the headless ghost mentioned in the treasure clues? And was that why the word *plunder* was used?

His excitement bubbled over and he flung off his bed sheets. He needed to tell somebody, anybody, what he'd discovered, but whom? Pablo was asleep and his parents would have a fit if he called this late. Marisol was also asleep and he couldn't call her. No way was he calling Susie Norris.

He crept up the basement stairs and stepped gingerly to his mother's computer in the living room. He turned on the computer and shot an email to Charlotte: *I think I've made some progress on the clues. Think famous pirates.*

He knew there was no way that Charlotte could still be awake at this late hour, but he figured she'd see the email in the morning. He felt like he could finally get to sleep now and crept down the basement stairs, slipped into bed, and fell asleep. Had he still been at his mother's computer, he would have seen an email from Charlotte marked *Urgent* and sent to his Inbox: *Jeffrey, call me as soon as you get this! Important!*

Chapter 19

"Jeffrey, over here!" Marisol waved her arm over her head in the crowded cafeteria.

Carrying his lunch tray, Jeffrey zigzagged his way through the crowd to Marisol's table. He set his tray down and slid in across from her.

"I've been looking for you," Marisol said.

"I've been looking for *you*," Jeffrey replied. "I think I've made some progress on the treasure clues."

Marisol's eyes lit up. "You're kidding."

Jeffrey glanced left and right. Satisfied that no one could hear him, he leaned across the table and spoke in a low tone. "I think the part that goes, *See kings plunder the headless ghost* is talking about Blackbeard the pirate."

Marisol stared back at him, wide-eyed.

"When Blackbeard was killed," Jeffrey continued, "his head was cut off and hung from the front of the ship. Ever since then there's been a famous legend about his headless ghost."

Marisol slapped both palms down on the table. "Jeffrey, that's fantastic! That's why it says the word *plunder*!"

"Yes!" Jeffrey practically shouted. "That's exactly what I thought!" He grinned at Marisol and saw her grinning back.

A lunch tray slid across the table between them. They

looked up to see Susie. "Marisol, I've been waiting to talk to you all day." Susie plopped herself down on a seat and popped French fries in her mouth. "Where have you been? There's a new guy in my math class named Bradley. He looks just like that guy in the movie we saw last week. Look! There he is! The tall one with the spiky hair. Oh, and did you see what Debbie Wolf did to her hair? I can't believe it. She looks so tacky. By the way, can I borrow your history notes? I'm totally lost on that last chapter. I don't know why we have to have a quiz every Friday. If you ask me, it's totally unfair. I mean, come on, can't they give us a little time to process the information? Oh, and one more thing – " Susie noticed Jeffrey staring at her with a simmering look, and she froze with a French fry in hand, midway between her plate and her mouth. "What?"

"We were having a conversation," Jeffrey said.

"Oh. Well fill me in. I'm all ears."

"A private conversation," Jeffrey told her.

"Private, my you-know-what! Is this about that missing treasure?"

"Maybe it is, and maybe it isn't," Jeffrey said cryptically. He leaned back in his seat and folded his arms across his chest.

"Then maybe you better tell me. I know when you're up to something, Jeffrey Jones, and you're up to something."

"Why should I tell you anything?" Jeffrey said, his anger

rising. "You gave me a hard time just yesterday about being grounded, and now you want to get involved again? No way!"

Susie rose out of her seat and her voice rose with her. "Is this about the treasure or isn't it? Because if it is, let me tell you something –"

"Tell me what?" Jeffrey demanded, rising himself.

"Guys, shhh!" Marisol cautioned.

Jeffrey glanced around. A sea of curious faces stared back at him. He slid sheepishly back in his seat.

Susie slid back in hers, leaned over the lunchroom table, and whispered harshly. "If this is about the treasure, then I'm entitled to hear every word, and you know it!"

"And just how do you figure that?" Jeffrey asked.

"I'll tell you how I figure it." Susie grabbed the end of her hair and thrust it forward. "You see this? My beautiful hair? Hair that girls envy and boys lust over? It was almost burnt to a crisp by that maniac who tied us all up. And just how do you think I'd look, walking around school with a blowtorch haircut? That man could have killed me and it would have been on your conscience, mister. Assuming he didn't kill you, too. And on top of all that, I'm still grounded, with no relief in sight. That's how I figure it. So if you have information about that treasure, spill it, 'cause I want to know!"

Jeffrey looked at Marisol. She shrugged.

"Well?" Susie said. "I'm waiting."

Pablo stepped up to the table. "Hey, guys." He slipped off

his backpack, and slid into an empty seat. "What did I miss?"

"Nothing," said Jeffrey.

"Everything," said Susie.

Pablo looked at them both and then at Marisol. Marisol held up her hands. "Don't look at me."

Jeffrey sighed. "All right, here's what I've come up with."

Susie clapped her hands. "Tell me, tell me, tell me!"

Jeffrey gave her a withering look, and then spoke to Pablo. "You know that part of the puzzle that talks about a headless ghost? I think it means Blackbeard the pirate."

"Yes!" Pablo said. "They cut off his head and hung it off the ship! And his headless ghost still haunts Ocracoke Island, searching for his missing head. Jeffrey, that makes total sense."

"I agree," said Marisol. "It's got to be Blackbeard, but what does it mean? And how can it lead us to the treasure?"

Jeffrey shook his head. "That's all I've got so far. I'm still trying to figure the rest out." He told Marisol and Susie about his talk with Charlotte's uncle, the murdered treasure hunter, and the crisis in Germany. "I looked on the internet and it's just like Markus said: Germany and large parts of Europe are under siege. Their own leaders have betrayed them, and their countries are being flooded with millions of foreign invaders. Women and children are being assaulted, men are being attacked and arrested; it's horrible. We can't let that fat man get his hands on the treasure and give it to the German government."

"Maybe I can help," Pablo said. "I went to the library on my free period and did some research on the computer." He reached for his backpack and pulled out a sheaf of papers. "The treasure hunter's name is Hermann Schmidt. I guess I should say his name *was* Hermann Schmidt since he's dead now. Check this out." He handed them each a copy of a news story he'd printed out at the school library.

Marisol read the headline: "Treasure Hunter Disappears."

Susie read the first two sentences: "German treasure hunter Hermann Schmidt disappeared without a trace last week. German authorities believe he made off with a stash of gold coins and artifacts valued at over two hundred million dollars." She turned to Marisol. "Two hundred million dollars!"

"Look down at the bottom," Pablo said.

Jeffrey's eyes scanned down the page to a grainy black and white photograph. The photo showed Hermann Schmidt, kneeling on the deck of a ship next to an open treasure chest. The chest overflowed with gold coins. Fanned out alongside of him were eight other men, identified in the caption as divers, crewmen and investors.

"Look at the third guy on the left," Pablo said.

Jeffrey counted three people over and saw a husky man, wearing a broad smile and glasses. "It looks like the fat man,"

Jeffrey said.

"It is the fat man," Susie confirmed, "only he's younger in this picture. I'd recognize that grubby face anywhere."

"That was the original crew that discovered the sunken ship," Pablo said.

Marisol turned to him. "So the German man who tied us up was a partner of this treasure hunter, Hermann Schmidt."

"Looks that way," Pablo said.

Jeffrey looked up from his paper with a gleam in his eye. "Pablo, did you get the fat man's name? Charlotte's uncle wouldn't tell me."

Pablo shook his head. "The only name the article mentions is Hermann Schmidt's. He was the leader. But I did find another article." He passed out another round of papers. "The first page is a news story on Schmidt's family. He left a wife and three kids behind in Germany when he disappeared. As you know, they were all murdered."

Marisol and Susie read the article silently. Jeffrey skimmed it. This, too, was exactly as Charlotte's uncle Markus had described it: Hermann Schmidt's family was tortured with a blowtorch and then shot in the head. Based on Jeffrey's experience with the fat man, it seemed likely that he was the killer.

"The next page is the obituary for Hermann Schmidt," Pablo said. "His body was found in a gutter here in Los Angeles. His throat was cut."

Susie gasped. "This is terrible."

Pablo shrugged and leaned back in his chair. "Somebody is really out to get that treasure."

"I'd sure like to get that fat man's name," Jeffrey said.

"Give me some more time," Pablo told him. "I might be able to find it. I'll go to the library tonight after football practice. My dad says I can still go to the library."

"I'll go with you," Marisol said. "I can go to the library, too."

"Sounds good," Jeffrey said. "I'll keep working on the treasure clues."

"What about me?" Susie asked eagerly. "What do I do?"

"You stay home and take care of your precious hair," Jeffrey said.

Marisol laughed.

Susie's face turned beet red. "If you think you're going to keep me off this investigation, let me tell you, you've got another think coming!"

"Calm down," Jeffrey said. "I was just joking. Why don't you work on the first part of the puzzle? The part about the clock. We know it has something to do with the location of the treasure."

"Alright, I'll work on that." Susie turned to Marisol. "Just think, Marisol: this treasure is worth two hundred million dollars. We could buy a lot of shoes with that money."

Jeffrey and Pablo laughed, but Marisol's look was serious.

She laid her papers down on the lunch table and tapped them with her finger. "I have a feeling we might all be better off if we never find this treasure."

"Why do you say that?" Susie asked.

Marisol met Susie's gaze, and then looked soberly at Jeffrey and Pablo. "Because," she answered, "so far everyone who's had anything to do with this treasure has ended up dead."

Chapter 20

"Treasure, you say? What's this about a treasure?"

Jeffrey and Pablo were back in Mr. Beasley's living room. Once again, it was warm. And once again, Mr. Beasley lay sprawled across the sofa, impeccably dressed in a wool suit. Though he still sported a cast on his left leg, his neck brace was gone and his face looked much better. The boys sat across from him in stiff-backed chairs.

The meeting had begun with great excitement. They told him about their adventure in tracking down the mysterious gray Porsche, and they gave him the car's license plate number and the pictures Susie took of the car. Mr. Beasley was duly impressed, and true to his word, had paid Jeffrey and Pablo each a hundred dollars as a reward. "I only hope that the police can use your information to track down the driver," he had said, before adding, "But I doubt they will."

Next was the tale of their dangerous encounter with the blowtorch-wielding fat man.

"Monstrous!" Mr. Beasley had exclaimed. However, at the mention of the word "treasure," he had perked up considerably.

"It's gold that was recovered from a sunken Spanish galleon," Jeffrey explained. "At least, that's what we've been told."

"And this Schmidt fellow," said Mr. Beasley, "this treasure hunter, he absconded with it, did he?"

"He hid it somewhere," Pablo said, "and then he croaked."

"How unfortunate," said Mr. Beasley.

"He was murdered," Jeffrey said, and then he told Mr. Beasley about the letter that Hermann Schmidt had mailed to his family containing clues to the treasure's location.

If not for the cast on his leg, Mr. Beasley would have leapt off the couch. "He left you clues?"

The boys nodded.

Mildred Beasley entered carrying a silver tray laden with a tea kettle and three cups. The tea filled the air with a warm, pungent smell and made the room feel even muggier than it already was. Jeffrey placed a finger on the center of his glasses and slid them back up his nose. Pablo, starting to sweat, tugged at his collar. Mildred set the tray on the coffee table.

"Mildred," said Mr. Beasley, "our guests have told me the most extraordinary news. They're on the trail of a treasure in missing gold."

Mildred stiffened and seemed to pale. "Oh, dear.... Please tell me it isn't so."

"It is so. And it's all connected to that ghastly gray Porsche that almost did me in."

"Herbert," said his wife, "I don't want you getting

involved in this kind of talk. You're in no condition to go on a treasure hunt."

"Confound it, woman, I'm only listening. Surely, there's no harm in that."

"Yes, listening now and acting later. Now I'm not going to argue with you. I insist you drop any and all talk about a treasure this very instant."

Jeffrey and Pablo exchanged a bewildered look.

Mr. Beasley caught it and said, "Men, I know a thing or two about treasures. You see, I was an amateur treasure hunter in my youth."

"In your youth and beyond," Mildred sniffed. "Why, when I think about all the money you've wasted on those ridiculous treasure hunts of yours, I could just scream." She picked up the kettle and poured tea into the cups.

"We went to Jamaica for two weeks," she told the boys, "and he spent the entire time up and down the beach with that silly contraption of his, looking for treasure."

"It's not a contraption," Mr. Beasley grumbled, "It's a metal detector." He looked at the boys. "You never know what you're going to find buried under the sand on a foreign beach."

Mildred set the tea kettle back on the tray with a stiff clink. "That trip cost us a month's salary and you know what he found? Nothing. Absolutely nothing."

"Correction, Mildred. I found a license plate and two

small coins."

"What a genius!" Mildred looked at the boys. "Another time we went to Australia. Same thing. Up and down the beach he goes. Didn't find a thing."

"Mildred, you're boring our guests and once again you stand corrected. I found a silver dollar buried in the sand on our trip to Australia. In fact, I still have it."

"Well, what a brainy one you are. Spend three thousand dollars for a holiday and come back with one dollar."

She shook her head and handed a cup of tea to Pablo. Pablo thanked her and wondered if it was the same foul-tasting tea she had served them the last time they were there. He took a sip. It was.

"I'm afraid Mildred is not the adventurous type," Mr. Beasley said.

"I'm not the stupid type is what you mean." She turned away from Pablo and handed a cup of tea to Jeffrey, and then one to her husband. With no one watching, Pablo turned to a tall potted plant at his side and quietly poured his tea into the soil.

Mildred turned back to face him and saw his empty cup. "Good heavens, drank all your tea that fast? Let's have your cup." Pablo forced a smile as she refilled his cup with tea.

"Never mind the tea," Mr. Beasley said. "Let's talk about the treasure."

"Herbert, what did I just tell you?" his wife huffed. "I

don't want you getting involved in any kind of treasure nonsense."

"Relax, dear. I'm merely curious."

"Yes, and curiosity killed the cat. Remember that." She picked up her tray and stalked out of the room.

"Thank goodness," Mr. Beasley muttered.

"I heard that!" Mildred called from the kitchen.

Mr. Beasley rolled his eyes.

From the kitchen: "Did he tell you about the time he went to jail for his treasure hunting?"

The boys sat up straight in their chairs. "You went to jail, Mr. Beasley?" Pablo asked.

The teacher flushed a deep red. "I was detained and released."

Mildred stepped in from the kitchen. "He was *arrested* and released," she said. "For trespassing. Him." She wagged a finger at her husband and stepped back in the kitchen.

"It's a long story," Mr. Beasley explained. "I thought I'd try my luck treasure hunting on a private beach, but the locals would have none of it."

Mildred called from the kitchen, "Signs were posted clear as day: No Trespassing."

Mr. Beasley snapped at the kitchen, "Thank you, Mildred, for that scintillating observation." He lowered his voice and whispered to the boys. "Mildred doesn't understand, but when one is on a treasure hunt, all propriety goes out the window." He glanced at the kitchen to make sure his wife had not heard, and then turned back to Jeffrey and Pablo with an eager eye. "Now about this treasure ..."

Pablo told Mr. Beasley about the research he'd done and handed him copies of the news stories about Hermann Schmidt. Mr. Beasley read them over, and then Jeffrey told him about the treasure clues and added, "I think the part about the headless ghost is talking about Blackbeard the pirate. When he was killed his head was cut off and hung from the bow of a ship. That's why the word *plunder* is used. It's a clue that the headless ghost is a pirate."

Jeffrey watched anxiously as Mr. Beasley digested what he'd just said. He thought his Blackbeard deduction was a good one and he was eager to hear his teacher's approval.

Mr. Beasley took a deep breath and said, "That's all quite interesting, and you've both shown a remarkable application of intellect. However, I detect one major flaw in your line of reasoning concerning those treasure clues. Two flaws, actually."

"What flaws?" Pablo asked.

"You said that the letter this man Schmidt sent to his family in Germany was mailed from Los Angeles, correct?"

"That's right," said Pablo.

"As far as we know, it's right," Jeffrey added.

"Very well, then that means the treasure is likely here, somewhere in this city or close by. However, Blackbeard never set foot in California. He sailed the Atlantic Ocean and the Caribbean, and he was killed off the North Carolina coast. Indeed, the legend of his headless ghost is specifically confined to Ocracoke Island. If this man Schmidt wanted his family to find his treasure, then it is highly unlikely that he would include a clue that might send them in the wrong direction."

Jeffrey sat perfectly still. "What's the second flaw?"

"If Schmidt was an experienced treasure hunter, and he must have been in order to find the wreckage of that Spanish galleon, then surely he knew that the notion of buried treasure is a literary myth. Indeed, the only historical pirate known to bury treasure was Captain Kidd. Real pirates didn't bury treasure. I'm surprised you don't know that, Jones."

Jeffrey cringed. He did know it.

Mr. Beasley continued. "That makes it even more unlikely that Blackbeard or any pirate is the answer to one of the clues. A man of Schmidt's intellect must have known that such clues would only confuse the very people he intended to help find his treasure. It seems to me that these hints of pirates and Blackbeard's ghost may have been deliberately intended as false leads."

Jeffrey felt his stomach twist into a knot. His entire premise had just unraveled before his eyes. Worst of all, he should have known better. He knew about Blackbeard and pirates. He had stayed up half the night reading about them.

Was he losing his power of deduction?

Pablo eyed his friend with concern. "You okay, Jeffrey? You look real pale, man."

Jeffrey took a deep breath and nodded. "I'm fine. I just – I thought my analysis was correct, but obviously it's not. I guess I'll just have to start over."

"Wait a second," Pablo said. "Maybe you are right." He looked at Mr. Beasley. "You could be wrong, couldn't you, Mr. Beasley?"

Jeffrey waved away the idea. "No, he's right. His analysis makes perfect sense. It's my theory that's incorrect."

Mr. Beasley straightened himself on the couch as best he could. "Now look here, Jones. Don't feel bad about being wrong on a clue. After all, if this treasure hunting business was easy, everyone would be doing it. I've seen enough of you to know that you're quite capable of solving this mystery. I dare say, I can't think of anyone more capable. Both of you, in fact. You and young Mr. Reyes make a formidable team."

Pablo grinned. "Thanks, Mr. Beasley."

Jeffrey didn't answer. He kicked himself in his mind. How could he have been so stupid? Worst of all, he knew Charlotte would be disappointed.

Charlotte was disappointed.

Jeffrey could hear it in her voice over the phone. "What

do we do now?" she asked him.

"Well, I have to start over, that's all," he told her. "I'm good at puzzles and figuring stuff out."

Charlotte sighed. "I know you are, Jeffrey. I just didn't think it was going to take this long."

"Neither did I," Jeffrey admitted. Then, stealing a line from Mr. Beasley, he added, "But after all, if this treasure hunting business was easy, everyone would be doing it."

Charlotte laughed, and for the first time since he and Pablo had met with their teacher, Jeffrey didn't feel like a complete loser.

Chapter 21

Saturday morning found Jeffrey and Pablo back in the musty church basement, helping Father Pat pack supplies for the church missions.

The boys loaded cans of chicken soup into cardboard boxes, sealed the boxes tight with packing tape, and told the priest about their success in tracking down the gray Porsche, their encounter with the sinister fat man, and the clues to the treasure.

"It sounds like an interesting case," mused Father Pat, "but also a dangerous one, don't you think?"

Pablo drew himself up straight as a spear. "No worries, Father. Danger is my middle name."

Father Pat let out a hearty laugh. He shook his head as if to clear it, then he looked at the boys and the lines on his face grew serious. "All the same, Pablo, you should know that the gold you're seeking comes with a history. A history of unspeakable horror and violence."

"What do you mean, Father?" Pablo asked.

"I'm talking about the Aztec Indians and the founding of Mexico by Hernan Cortes."

"We read about that in school," Pablo said.

"Then it's doubtful you've heard the whole story." Father Pat sank wearily onto a wooden bench and stretched out his legs. "And what a story it is: romance, danger, adventure, heroism. It's all there."

Jeffrey and Pablo exchanged knowing looks. Father Pat was about to tell them a story. They cleared boxes off a couple of chairs, pulled the chairs up, and leaned in close as the priest began his tale.

"At the time of Columbus," said Father Pat, "the Islamic slave traders controlled the Arabian Sea, stretching from East Africa to Asia. When Columbus set sail, he wasn't looking for America; he was looking for an alternate trade route to India. That's why he called the natives he found 'Indians.' He didn't know that he'd just discovered a new continent. He thought he'd landed in the Far East."

"Boy, was he in for a surprise," Pablo said.

"He sure was. So was Spain. So was all of Europe. Columbus was a complicated man. On the one hand, there's evidence that he may have been a slave-holder. On the other hand, he praised the first natives he encountered for their beauty, their generosity, and their intelligence. That's why he was horrified when he returned to America on a second voyage and found that the men he'd left behind had been murdered and cannibalized."

"Cannibalized?" Pablo said.

"Eaten for lunch."

Pablo shuddered. "I'm glad we weren't there."

"That makes two of us," said Father Pat. "The Arawak

Indians who ate Columbus's men were fond of human flesh. However, as bad as cannibalism is, it was nothing compared to the horrors the Spanish encountered among the Aztecs."

Father Pat studied the two boys. His jaw tightened and the deep creases on his face seemed to quiver. It was a look that Jeffrey recognized from his own father; the look his father always had when he wasn't sure whether Jeffrey was old enough or mature enough to handle the truth he was about to tell him. Jeffrey knew that Father Pat was debating in his mind whether or not to tell them about the gruesome history of the Aztec Empire.

The priest took a deep breath and began. "When Hernan Cortes and his men first met the Aztec Indians and their surrounding tribes in Mexico in 1519, they were witness to an evil straight from the gates of Hell." He paused and looked at each of the two boys in turn, his eyes boring into theirs. "Human sacrifice."

Pablo squirmed in his seat. "No way, man."

"Yes way, man. The Aztecs practiced human sacrifice. Their ceremonies began with shrieks, whistles, and thunderous drumbeats; incessant, intoxicating drumbeats. Then the victims, mainly children and Indians who were captured from other tribes, were marched up the stone steps of the altar and held down over the slabs. It took four Indian priests to hold the victim down, one for each arm and leg. While the victim screamed, a fifth priest raised a jagged knife and plunged it into the victim's chest. The priest tore out the still-beating heart and held it aloft, gushing blood, for the shrieking crowds to see. Then the priest cut off the victim's head, legs, and arms. The heads were impaled on sticks, and the arms and legs were cooked and eaten."

The boys sat riveted. "They were cannibals, too?" Pablo asked.

"Yes, and they considered young children a particular delicacy."

Pablo winced.

Father Pat took another deep breath. "The Aztecs slaughtered their victims by the thousands, one after the other, until the priests collapsed from exhaustion. They performed over twenty thousand sacrifices a year, mainly children and babies, cutting out their hearts and then eating the bodies."

"My history teacher, Mrs. Daniels, told us the Aztecs were peaceful people, practicing their native culture," Jeffrey said. "She calls it moral relativism."

Father Pat shook his head. "Jeffrey, when I hear nonsense like that, I don't know whether to laugh or cry. I know Nancy Daniels, she's a member of this parish, and she means well, but her liberal education has turned her mind to mush."

The boys chuckled and shifted uneasily in their chairs. It was a stilted laugh, tinged by the gruesome images Father

Pat had just painted in their minds.

"The Aztecs were an empire of pure incontestable evil," Father Pat said, "and Cortes and the Spaniards saw it as their sacred duty to Christianize them. They warned the Indians before every battle and offered them peace if they would only give up their wicked ways and embrace God, but the Indians refused."

"They warned the Indians before they attacked?" Pablo asked.

"They sure did. By order of the Spanish crown, known as the *requerimiento*, Cortes and his men read a solemn declaration before every battle except Cholulan, where the Spaniards were led into a trap. They told the Aztecs repeatedly that violence wasn't necessary, and that they could live and work together in peace, but the Indians insisted on fighting."

"They never told us any of this in school," Pablo said.

"Of course not," said Father Pat. "History is written in blood, not ink; and schools love nothing more than rewriting history. Of all the Indian tribes in Mexico, the Aztecs were the most feared and the most powerful. Cortes and his men spent months in the Aztec capital, begging their king, Montezuma, to give up their serpent god and their practice of human sacrifice, but just when it appeared that Montezuma was ready to embrace peace with the Spaniards, he was stoned to death by his own people, and a full scale war was on. The Aztecs outnumbered the Spanish army over ten thousand to one. They fought the Spaniards with darts, spears, arrows, and rocks. And yet, battle after battle, the Spaniards emerged victorious and eventually prevailed."

"How did they do it?" Pablo asked.

"It was a miracle, Pablo; an act of Divine Providence. God used Cortes and his men to put an end to human sacrifice and cannibalism, and to bring Christianity to the New World. The Spaniards laid the groundwork for the coming of Our Lady of Guadalupe in 1531."

Pablo smiled. "Ah, Guadalupe!"

"You know the story," said Father Pat. "Mary, the mother of Jesus, appeared to Juan Diego and imprinted her image on his cloak. It was a powerful image for the Aztecs and it led to the peaceful conversion of tens of millions of Indians to the Christian faith."

"I have the picture at home," Pablo said.

"Good for you."

"Mrs. Daniels says she doesn't believe in Guadalupe," Jeffrey said.

Father Pat scowled. "Your teacher is a damn fool. Excuse my language, but she is. The tilma of Guadalupe has been examined by scientists from all over the world and proven to be of supernatural origin. You know what that means? It means it's real."

A sense of wonder filled the priest's voice. "It's one of the most incredible miracles in the history of mankind, the actual image of the mother of Jesus, still immaculate after five hundred years! Just think of it, millions upon millions of souls saved for Heaven, and it all began with the strength of one man: Hernan Cortes."

"What about gold?" Pablo asked.

"Oh, there was plenty of gold, no doubt about it. And the Spaniards took their fill. Most of it came from neighboring tribes. The Aztecs had terrorized their Indian neighbors for so long that many of them joined the Spaniards in their fight. When the Spanish army defeated the Aztecs, their Indian allies showered them with gold. So you see, this treasure you're chasing is both holy and cursed. It's holy by the conversion of the Aztecs and other Indians from a culture of death to a culture of life. It's cursed by the blood of human sacrifice and cannibalism that preceded it."

The boys were in a somber mood walking home. They walked slowly, studying the cracks in the sidewalk in front of them.

"Do you think that treasure has a curse on it?" Pablo asked. Before Jeffrey could respond, Pablo added, "Because if it does, then maybe Marisol is right and we should just leave it alone."

"I hate to stop now," Jeffrey said. "That fat man is going

to keep killing people until he finds it."

"Maybe we just need a vacation from it, huh? Marisol wants to go to the carnival tonight."

Jeffrey nodded. "That's good. You should go."

"She wants all of us to go: You, me, her, and Susie."

Jeffrey stopped walking and stared at Pablo. "No way! I'm not taking Susie Norris anywhere."

"Don't worry," Pablo said, "I got it all figured out: me and Marisol, and you and Charlotte."

Chapter 22

The carnival tents and trailers were garishly colored, and the neon lights of the rides shone brilliantly in the night sky, calling like sirens from the local park.

Only a stone's throw from Jeffrey's house, the fall carnival was an annual tradition for both him and Pablo, but this was the first time they had company attending. Marisol walked with them from Jeffrey's house, and then the three of them met Charlotte by the park entrance.

They circled behind the rides, accompanied by the rumbling sound of motors and generators, and emerged at the far end of the midway. It was a path Jeffrey and Pablo had taken many times before, and it placed them squarely in front of the ticket cage. A woman with frizzy, gray-streaked hair and glasses sat inside. Her eyebrows arched as they stepped up to the window and her face said, "Well?"

"Four tickets to the Tilt-A-Whirl," Pablo said, sliding a ten dollar bill across the counter.

The woman pushed back four red tickets and change. "Ferris wheel?"

"Nah."

"Carnival ain't a carnival without a ride on the wheel."

"Alright," Pablo said. "Give us the Ferris wheel. Give us everything."

The nighttime air was crisp and smelled of hot dogs and cotton candy. They strolled down the midway, past the screams and scurrying of young children. Teenagers swarmed around them, older Latino boys with shaved heads and flannel shirts buttoned up to their necks, and Latina girls dressed in skinny jeans, their faces slathered in makeup, each one indistinguishable from the next. There were day laborers with their families, and an assortment of vagrants that came drawn to the bright lights of the carnival like moths to a flame.

Rock music blared from the Himalaya ride, squeals and rubber thumps echoed from the bumper cars, and all around them were the beckoning calls of the carnival barkers: "Win a prize for the lady! Anyone can play this game! Hey, mister, how about you?"

"Let's forget about the treasure for one night and just have fun," Marisol said. She surrendered her red ticket to a teenaged ride jockey with a ring in his ear, and climbed into a car on the Tilt-A-Whirl.

"Sounds good to me," Pablo said. He slid in next to Marisol, grinning from ear to ear.

"Me too," said Jeffrey, but he knew there was no way he could forget about the treasure, not even for a second. For Jeffrey, their hunt for the treasure was much more exciting than being strapped into a metal cage and spun silly on a carnival ride. He and Charlotte took the next car, the Tilt-A-

Whirl snapped into action, and they all screamed as the ride whipped them around in a kaleidoscope of colors.

They climbed down from the Tilt-A-Whirl, feeling dizzy and rubbery-legged. A swirling blur of lights, faces, and carnival attractions spun in circles around them. "Let's go again!" Marisol cried.

They rode the Zoomer, the bumper cars, and then the Ferris wheel, which lifted them back and up in a wide, smooth-flowing arc. Seated next to Jeffrey, Charlotte's golden hair fluttered in the breeze and her eyes sparkled. Each time they passed over the top, Jeffrey pointed to a familiar building and exclaimed, "There's my house! There's my school! There's my church!"

At one point, the wheel creaked to a stop, leaving them poised at the very tippy-top of the ride. Seemingly above the clouds, they could see for miles and the world spread out before them, looking small and insignificant.

Charlotte swept her arm across the twinkling lights of the city. "All this could be ours, Jeffrey."

Jeffrey blinked. "How do you figure?"

"If you could find that missing treasure, we'd be rich and then all this would be ours."

"I'm doing the best I can."

"I know you are," she said, and laced her fingers around his.

Jeffrey's heart skipped. Her fingers felt smooth, cool and

soft. They fell silent, holding hands. Charlotte pressed close to him and laid her head on his shoulder, gazing dreamily out over the city. Jeffrey stared straight ahead. The wheel lurched forward, carrying them down in a slow descent. It stopped at the bottom and they released hands. Nobody had seen. They climbed out of their car. Pablo and Marisol, who had already disembarked, stood waiting for them.

"Where to now?" Marisol asked, her smile wide and her eyes gleaming.

Before anyone could answer, a voice boomed from the crowd: "Jones!" Jeffrey and his friends turned their heads to the sound. Across the midway, Brian McHugh waved his arms in the air. "Jones!"

"Who's that?" Charlotte asked.

"Trouble," said Pablo.

"What kind of trouble?"

"You'll see."

Brian started towards them, bulling his way forward. The crowd parted like the Red Sea to let him pass. A girl followed behind him, hurrying to keep pace. She was their age, but looked older with lipstick, teased hair, and gobs of makeup.

"Jones!" Brian hollered. More people scattered.

"Be careful, Jeffrey," Charlotte whispered.

Pablo braced and clenched his right hand into a fist. Marisol laid her hand on top of his. "Don't fight, Pablo," she whispered.

"It'll be hard not to," Pablo whispered back. "All he ever wants to do is fight."

Brian was a hulk of a boy, as tall as Pablo, but twice as wide. He strode up to them and planted himself in front of the shorter Jeffrey. The girl trailing Brian caught up and slouched behind him, chewing gum and trying to look tough.

"Didn't you hear me, man?" Brian said. "I called you like six times."

"We heard you," Pablo replied. "What do you want?"

"I'm not talking to you, Reyes."

"I'm talking to you."

Brian's ears burned red and flared out from the side of his head. Jeffrey spoke quickly. "I heard you, Brian. What is it?"

Brian kept his eyes on Pablo a moment longer, and then turned back to Jeffrey. "Jones, I need your help."

"*My* help?" Jeffrey was shocked.

Brian looked suddenly sheepish. "That professor guy, over by the sideshow tent, he took all my money."

Pablo stifled a laugh. Marisol squeezed his arm. Brian heard the laugh and glared. "It ain't funny, Reyes."

"I'm not laughing," Pablo said, trying his best to keep a straight face.

"How did he take your money?" Jeffrey asked.

"If you stump him, you keep your money and win a prize, and I couldn't stump him."

"How much did you lose?"

"Twenty-five dollars."

Pablo couldn't help himself and burst into a laugh.

Brian clenched his fists. "It ain't funny, Reyes!"

"It's okay," Jeffrey said, reaching out to calm the bigger boy. "How do you want me to help you?"

"I need you to get my money back."

"How?"

"By stumping that professor."

"I don't even know who this professor guy is."

"I'll show you."

Leading them across the midway, Brian grew angrier with every step. His ears were burning red and flapped out so wide, a strong wind would have lifted him straight up in the air. "It's a rip-off!" he said. "A cheap carnival rip-off!"

They found the professor at the far end of the midway, perched atop a platform in front of the sideshow tent. He sat erect in a stiff-backed chair, a prim and proper man with a thin mustache and a tight-fitting suit. A crowd mingled before him. Behind the professor was a prize board covered with huge stuffed animals.

On the platform with the professor, strutted a carnival barker, a wiry little man with the face of a river rat and a voice like screeching pipes. "Step right up, folks! Stump the professor! Keep your money and win a prize! Who's next?"

Jeffrey and his friends watched from their little group. A husky woman in a pixie haircut and wearing a faded muumuu dress handed the barker a five dollar bill and looked up at the professor. "Name the state capitols."

Beginning with Montgomery, Alabama, the professor ran through the capitols of all fifty states. He spoke calmly, with a cultured voice, as if he were ordering tea and crumpets. He wasn't British, but he gave the impression that he was.

"How did you get mixed up with *this*?" Pablo asked Brian.

"I thought I could stump him by asking about baseball, but he knew all the answers. Then the madder I got, the more money I lost. I was out twenty-five dollars in no time. Who'd have figured a guy like that would know the starting lineups of every baseball team for the last twenty years?"

They watched as more would-be winners stepped up and peppered the professor with challenges. He rattled off answers to each and every one. Jeffrey watched carefully. Brian turned to him. "What do you think, Jones?"

"He sounds like a memory expert," Jeffrey observed. "But that doesn't mean he's able to think logically or even intelligently."

"I don't care about any of that. I just want to know if you can outsmart him."

"Jeffrey can outsmart anybody," Marisol said.

Charlotte's eyes flashed at Marisol's remark. She looked at Marisol, and then back to Jeffrey.

"I can't get your money back," Jeffrey told Brian, "but I might be able to win some prizes."

"That's all I want to know," Brian said. He turned to the girl who had trailed him and spoke in a low voice. "Darla, give me five dollars."

The request brought a look of horror. "*What*?"

"Come on, baby. I'm out of money, you know that."

Darla chewed her gum rapidly and looked at Brian askance. "So you want my five dollars now?"

"It's to win your prize, baby. Don't you want one of them big teddy bears?"

Darla looked up at the prize board filled with stuffed animals and popped her gum. Brian pointed his thumb back at Jeffrey. "See that guy? That chubby guy? Trust me, that guy is smart. He can win this thing."

The barker strutted like a rooster across the platform and gestured at the professor. "He's a walking, talking encyclopedia of knowledge, folks. Brighter than a thousand watt bulb. Who's next?"

Brian leaned in close to Darla. "Come on, baby. Please."

Darla wrinkled her nose. She slid two fingers into the hip pocket of her jeans and pulled out a crumpled five dollar bill. Brian snatched it immediately. "Hey!" she shouted.

"Here! Right here!" Brian called to the barker. He stepped towards the platform, waving Darla's money in the air.

The barker saw Brian approaching and smirked. "Back again, eh, genius?"

Brian slapped the bill in the barker's hand. "Not me," he

said. "Him." He pointed back at Jeffrey. "Come on, Jones."

A crowd of teenagers, construction workers, and middle-aged women watched as Jeffrey stepped forward. The barker eyed Jeffrey and nodded. "Go ahead, kid. Stump the professor. If you can."

Jeffrey looked up at the professor and said, "Mary's father has five daughters. The daughters are named Nana, Nene, Nini, and Nono. What's the name of the fifth daughter?"

The professor blinked. He was used to challenges that involved information and the recitation of facts. This one was different, still the answer was obvious. He sat up straight in his chair and cleared his throat. "The fifth daughter is named Nunu."

"Wrong," Jeffrey said. "If Mary's father has five daughters, then Mary is the fifth daughter."

A guffaw erupted from the crowd. Pablo, Marisol, and Charlotte cheered and clapped. Brian whooped and spun around. "Darla! What prize you want?"

Darla pointed up to a large snowy-white teddy bear. "That one."

Scowling, the barker reached for a long pole with a hook attached to the end of it and took down the white teddy bear. Brian grabbed the prize and ran it back to Darla. She squealed with delight.

The barker fished the five dollar bill out of his pocket and offered it back to Jeffrey. "Keep it," Jeffrey said. "I'm going again."

The barker hesitated and shot a look at the professor, who nodded curtly. "Okay, smart guy," the barker said to Jeffrey. "Go again."

Jeffrey looked up at the professor. "You're participating in a race and you just overtook the second place runner. What position are you in?"

The professor stared back at Jeffrey. "I am in first place."

"Wrong," Jeffrey said.

The barker cut in. "Wait a second. If he passes the second place runner, then he *is* in first place."

"No, he isn't," Jeffrey said. "If he overtakes the second place runner, then he's merely taken his place and he's now in second place. Another runner is still in first place."

"Yes!" Brian shouted. The crowd cheered and applauded. The professor threw up his hands.

Jeffrey pointed to a chocolate colored teddy bear on the prize board and said, "I'll take that one, please."

Muttering under his breath, the barker took down the prize and handed it to Jeffrey, along with the five dollar bill.

"Keep the money," Jeffrey said. "I'm going again."

"No, you're not," the barker replied.

"Let him go again!" Pablo shouted, followed by Marisol and Charlotte. The crowd took up the call. The barker stood with the bill in his hand. Jeffrey, holding the chocolate teddy bear, didn't budge.

Brian shouted up at the barker, "You took all my money, mister. Let him go again!"

The two men on the platform exchanged looks. The professor gave a small nod. "Alright, folks, calm down," the barker said. "He goes again." He waved his arm with a flourish. "Go ahead, wise guy. Stump the professor."

Jeffrey looked up at the professor. "A mute person goes into a shop and wants to buy a toothbrush. By pretending to brush his teeth, he communicates his intent to the shopkeeper and buys his toothbrush. Next, a blind man comes into the shop and wants to buy sunglasses. How does he indicate what he wants?"

The professor stared at Jeffrey and blinked. He started to answer, stopped, and began again. "The blind man shows the shopkeeper that he wants a pair of sunglasses."

"How?" Jeffrey asked.

"Like this." The professor imitated a blind man putting on glasses.

"Wrong," Jeffrey said. "The blind man opens his mouth and asks for it."

A roar went up from the crowd. Brian slapped Jeffrey on the back so hard it jostled his glasses. Pablo, Marisol, Charlotte, and Darla all cheered.

The barker yanked a red teddy bear off the prize board. "Alright, kid, that's enough. Here's your prize." He threw the teddy bear at Jeffrey. "And here's your money." He held the five dollar bill out for Jeffrey to take. "Now get out of here."

Jeffrey reached for the money, but Brian stopped him. "He's not finished," Brian told the barker.

"Yes, he is."

"No, he ain't." Brian turned to the crowd. "Are we finished?"

"No!" the crowd shouted. A pair of tough-looking young men stepped forward, dressed in gang attire and smelling of alcohol. "We ain't finished!" they yelled at the barker.

Jeffrey and Pablo shared a quick look. The barker backed away. "Now hold on folks," he said. "We run a respectable show here."

"Respectable enough to take my twenty-five dollars," Brian said.

"That's your own fault, son. You couldn't stump the professor."

Brian pointed back at Jeffrey. "He can."

The professor placed his hands on his thighs and rose from his seat.

"Where are you going?" the barker snapped.

The professor sighed. "You can continue without me. The boy is too smart." He slipped behind a curtain and disappeared.

The crowd booed and showered the barker with empty beer cans, wadded up paper balls, and debris. The barker ducked and the crowd surged forward. Pablo pushed his way through the crowd and grabbed Jeffrey by the arm. "Let's get out of here."

Brian intercepted them. "You can't go now! We got this guy on the ropes."

"We made our point," Jeffrey told him. He and Pablo pushed their way past the angry mob and back to Marisol and Charlotte. Jeffrey handed the chocolate teddy bear to Charlotte, the red one to Marisol, and they all hurried back toward the rides.

The angry crowd yelled and pounded their fists on the platform. Brian shouted up at the barker. "You owe me twenty-five dollars!"

The barker pulled a wad of bills from his pocket. With trembling hands, he peeled off twenty-five dollars and offered it to Brian. Brian snatched the money and ran back to Darla. The barker ducked behind the curtain.

The crowd screamed obscenities and seized hold of the platform, pushing and pulling. The structure wobbled and the wooden planks creaked and snapped.

"Jones!"

It was Brian. He and Darla ran down the midway and caught up with Jeffrey and his friends. "Jones, what's wrong with you? Why'd you run away like that?"

"You started a riot back there," Jeffrey said.

"So what?"

"So somebody could've been hurt," Marisol said.

"What do I care? I don't know those people."

"Man, that's messed up," Pablo said.

"Messed up? I got my money back!" He waved the twenty-five dollars in their faces.

"You should give it back," Pablo said.

"Are you crazy? You saw those guys, they're rip-offs!"

"You knew the rules before you played," Jeffrey said. "If you thought it wasn't fair, you shouldn't have played."

"Look who's talking." Brian pointed at the teddy bears that Marisol and Charlotte were holding. "You took your prizes."

"I won those prizes according to the rules of the game," Jeffrey said.

Brian's ears flared out. "So you're smart and I'm stupid, huh?"

"I'm not saying that."

"What's wrong with you? All of you? We could've cleaned out all their prizes!"

"Yeah, and then what?" Pablo said. "You had all those people ready to fight over some stupid stuffed animals."

"What do you care about those people for, Reyes? You don't know them from Adam."

Marisol held out her red teddy bear for Brian to take. "Here, you can have my prize. I don't want it."

Brian snatched the teddy bear. "Yeah, I'll take it if you

don't want it." He handed it to Darla, who now held two teddy bears. Brian nodded at Charlotte. "What about you?"

Charlotte hugged her teddy bear tightly against her chest. "I'm keeping mine."

Brian motioned to Darla. "Let's get out of here." To Jeffrey, he said, "I always knew you were weird, Jones, but this proves it." As he and Darla walked off, Brian called over his shoulder, "That's the last time I ever ask any of you for a favor."

"That's fine with us," Pablo called back.

They watched as Brian and Darla melded into the midway crowd and disappeared. "Greed," Jeffrey said. "It can turn anyone into a monster. I can't believe I fell for his stupid story. I'm just as guilty as he is."

The others lowered their heads, said nothing.

Across the midway, standing silently in the shadows and watching them closely, was Charlotte's uncle Markus.

Chapter 23

Jeffrey looked at himself in the mirror and hated what he saw.

Why did he do it? Why did he let himself get sucked into Brian's vendetta and cause such an ugly scene? He knew why. He thought he could impress Charlotte.

He turned away from the mirror and sat down at his desk. It was almost dawn. He had slept fitfully for a few hours before throwing off the bed sheets and turning on the light. Now he couldn't sleep at all. The ceiling above him creaked as his parents moved about the house, packing for their trip to San Diego.

He spread the treasure clues out on his desk and stared at the paper.

I am a hidden room. Approach my outer walls, find nothing. Look within. See kings plunder the headless ghost. One step beyond the grave.

Who was he kidding? The fat man couldn't solve the puzzle. The police, including Charlotte's uncle couldn't solve the puzzle. Who was he to think he could figure it out?

He stared at the words. That's all they were to him, just words. Might as well be Greek. He picked up a pencil and tapped it on the desktop. Words. Words that held the key to a golden treasure. A treasure valued at over two hundred million dollars. Words.

He noticed that the last letter of the word *room*, combined with the first two letters of the word that followed it, *approach*, spelled the word *map*. That's interesting, he thought. Here they were, searching for a hidden treasure, so a map would sure come in handy.

He started at the beginning and read the lines over again.

I am a hidden room. Approach my outer walls, find nothing. Look within. See kings plunder the headless ghost. One step beyond the grave.

As his eyes scanned over the words, he noticed something else peculiar. The word *see*, plus the first letter of the next word, *kings*, spelled the word *seek*. Like the word *map*, the word *seek* also seemed appropriate. After all, they were seeking a treasure.

He wondered if there was some sort of connection between the two words, or if it was just a coincidence. He read the lines again. Something drew his eyes to the word *plunder*. That was the word that first got him thinking about pirates. He studied the word, reading it forwards, backwards, and sideways. Almost as an afterthought, he noticed that if he removed the letters *p* and *l*, he was left with the word *under*.

Using his pencil, he wrote down the three words he had found: *map, seek, under.*

He gazed at the words. Minutes ticked by. On a hunch,

his eyes zipped back to the opening lines:

I am a hidden room. Approach my outer walls, find nothing. Look within.

Could that be it? Could the key to the treasure's location be hidden within the words themselves?

His blood racing, he scanned the lines again and again. Other words began to pop out. By taking the last letter of the word *my*, and combining it with the first two letters of the following word, *outer*, he had the word *you*.

He also noticed the word *the*, sitting alone between the words *plunder* and *headless*. He added them to his list and wrote the words in sequence: *map, you, seek, under, the*. He nearly fell out of his chair.

Was there a map to the treasure? If so, it was under something, but under what? He read the last two lines over and over.

See kings plunder the headless ghost. One step beyond the grave.

He noticed that the word *headless* could be broken into two words: *head* and *less*. Did either word apply? He had a hunch that one of them did, but which one, and how?

The map was under the ... what? Under the what?

The word *ghost* jumped out at him. He stared at it hard. Under the ghost? How could a map be hidden under a ghost? It didn't make any sense. The previous words he'd found were all solid and concrete. It only made sense that the final part of the puzzle would follow suit.

See kings plunder the headless ghost. One step beyond the grave.

Within those words lay the key to the treasure.

His mind was buzzing now. He knew he was close, very close. Words and phrases flashed before his eyes. Under the what? Under the what?

Suddenly, it came to him, the final part of the puzzle!

By taking the last two letters of the word *ghost*, combined with the first two letters of the following word, *one*, he had the word *stone*. And by adding the word *head* from *headless*, he now had the words *head stone*!

His hands trembled as he wrote the words in sequence on his paper: *Map you seek under the headstone.*

"Eureka!" he shouted.

He bounced out of his chair and stared at the words on his paper. It was all so obvious now. And the tipoff was under his nose all the time: *I am a hidden room. Approach my outer walls, find nothing. Look within.*

He'd done the impossible. He'd discovered the key to a five-hundred-year-old treasure. But he still wasn't finished. There was a map to the treasure, hidden under a headstone, but where was the headstone? If it was located in a cemetery, which cemetery?

He heard the basement door open at the top of the stairs and his father's voice call down. "Jeffrey, get up here!"

He found his parents waiting for him in the living room. Their travel bags packed and ready.

"Trash?" his father said.

"I took it out already."

"Fish?"

"I feed them in the morning and again at night."

"Phone numbers?"

"On the refrigerator and on Mom's desk."

"Emergencies?"

"Call 9-1-1. Call you and Mom. Leave the house in a fire, stand in a doorway for an earthquake, go downstairs for a tornado. Your gun is loaded and locked in your desk drawer. The key is on a chain on the wall. It's for emergencies only, in case someone breaks in the house."

"Right, someone breaks in this house, you shoot first and ask questions later. Otherwise, you don't touch it."

"I won't."

"Jeffrey," said his mother, "there's food in the kitchen, but you'll have to make it yourself. Be careful with the stove. Don't burn anything. For God's sake, don't burn the house down."

"I won't."

"And your room ..."

"I'll straighten up."

"I don't want you leaving the house, except for church," his father said. "Your friends can come over, but keep them in your room, not running all over the place. No parties. No loud music. And most of all," his father held up a finger for emphasis, "most of all: don't do anything stupid."

Jeffrey stared at his father.

"Did you hear me, Jeffrey?"

"I'm not stupid."

"I didn't say you were stupid. I said don't *do* anything stupid."

"I won't."

"Good. Then we're on the same page. We'll see you tonight."

His father extended his hand, and he and Jeffrey shook. His mother gave him a hug and a pat on the back. Then his parents picked up their bags and stepped out the front door. He heard their footsteps as they walked across the front porch.

Jeffrey pulled back the heavy drapes and watched from the living room window. Outside it was still dark. His parents loaded their bags in the trunk of the family car, got in, and backed out the driveway. The car rolled into the street and its brake lights flared. His parents looked and saw Jeffrey's face in the window. His father tapped the car horn twice, his mother smiled and gave a little wave, and they drove off.

Jeffrey watched until the car turned the corner and disappeared, and then he continued to stare out the window at the empty street. Behind him, the aquarium gurgled and bubbled, and his world seemed suddenly quiet. He had the house to himself, and he had a mystery to solve.

Chapter 24

"Whoa, what happened down here?"

Standing in the middle of Jeffrey's basement room that evening, Pablo couldn't believe what his own eyes were telling him. Jeffrey's books, constantly overflowing from his bookcase, were neatly stacked and put away. Jeffrey's clothes, normally strewn across his bed or draped over the nearest chair, were pressed and hung in orderly fashion in his closet. Jeffrey's bed, which only seemed to get made when his mother changed the bedding, was immaculate in appearance, with tightly fitted sheets and a clean bedspread.

"My mom made me clean it," Jeffrey said, looking sheepish. Dressed in a bright red shirt, he arranged chairs around the room. The upstairs doorbell rang. "Come in!" he yelled up the basement stairs.

Marisol and Susie entered the house and clattered down the stairs. They reached the basement and Susie stood gawking. "What happened down here?"

Pablo laughed. "That's what I said."

"Don't tell me you finally cleaned up this mess," Susie gushed. "It's the end of the world as we know it." She turned and saw Jeffrey standing awkwardly in his new red shirt. "And that shirt, Jeffrey, ooh la la!"

Pablo and Marisol laughed. Jeffrey's face flushed as red

as the shirt he was wearing. Marisol noticed his discomfort and gave Jeffrey a pat on the shoulder. "I like it, Jeffrey. It looks good on you."

"Please, don't encourage him," Susie said.

"It *does* look good on him," Marisol insisted.

Susie gazed about the room. "Look, I can see the floor. I can see the walls. It's a miracle."

The doorbell rang and Jeffrey was thankful for the interruption. He shouted up the basement stairs, "Come in!"

They heard the front door open and someone enter the house.

"Down here!" Jeffrey called.

Footsteps descended the basement stairs, followed by a pair of female legs, and then Charlotte in a short summer skirt. She carried a purse over her shoulder and she smiled wide when she saw Jeffrey. "Did you really solve the treasure clues?"

Jeffrey smiled back. "Not the whole thing, but we're close."

They all took seats and Jeffrey passed out copies of the treasure clues in which he'd circled the letter combinations he'd found. He watched their faces as they read his circled words: *map you seek under the headstone.*

Marisol gasped. Charlotte practically leapt out of her chair. "Jeffrey, you did it!"

"Not quite. There are still some clues we need to puzzle

out. If there is a map we still don't know what headstone it's under or what cemetery it's in. And we've forgotten all about the first clue. Remember that one?"

"I was working on that," Susie said. *"I'm wrong, but I could be right. Catch me twice if you can.* You said it was a clock."

"Right," Jeffrey said. "Because that clue came first I think it's meant to tell us the name or location of the cemetery where the map is located. Something to do with a clock. Any ideas? The floor is open."

Susie pulled out her phone. "I'll look for a cemetery with the name clock in it."

"I've already done that," Jeffrey said, "on my mom's computer. I couldn't find anything."

"What about a morgue or a place where bodies go before they get buried?" Pablo asked.

Jeffrey shook his head. "I tried that, too. No luck."

Susie shot her hand in the air. "I got it! According to the puzzle, it's not just any clock, it's a stopped clock. That's why it says 'catch me *twice* if you can.' Stopped clocks are right twice a day."

Jeffrey watched her carefully. "Yeah.... Go on."

"Well then the answer is obvious, it's a place where they take broken or stopped clocks. A graveyard for dead clocks: a clock repair shop."

Jeffrey and his friends sat in stunned silence. "That's

either a brilliant idea," Jeffrey said, "or the dumbest thing I've ever heard."

The others laughed.

Susie bubbled with excitement. "Of course, it's brilliant, don't you see? It makes perfect sense for the puzzle."

Marisol clapped her hands. "Susie, it's great!"

"What about the headstone?" Jeffrey said. "The map is supposed to be under a headstone."

"We have a grandfather clock in our living room," Susie explained, "and there's an inscription on the back. Maybe that's what it means by headstone. Or maybe it means the top of the clock. They call the front of the clock its face, so the top could be its head." She looked at the others around her. "Come on, guys, think outside the box."

Jeffrey frowned. He took off his glasses, rubbed his eyes, and put his glasses back on. Finally, he shook his head. "It's a clever idea, Susie, and very creative, but I think we're better off concentrating on cemeteries, at least to start. We can always come back to your idea later."

"Jeffrey, you're missing the point," Susie said.

Charlotte shot her a look. "I don't think he's missing the point at all. I think he's right."

Susie did a double take. "Wait, what?"

"I like the idea about a graveyard for dead clocks," Jeffrey said, "but it doesn't quite fit. I'll tell you what — "

Susie bobbed in her seat, waving her arms and cutting

him off. "Jeffrey, wait! Hear me out on this!"

"Why don't you let Jeffrey talk?" Charlotte said.

"Excuse me?" Susie exclaimed.

"You said your piece about clocks and Jeffrey answered you. The least you could do is let him finish what he's saying before interrupting him."

"Take it easy, guys," Pablo said.

Susie stared at Charlotte, and then turned back to Jeffrey. "I thought this was a meeting to try and find a treasure."

"It is," Jeffrey assured her.

"Then let me make my point."

"You made your point," said Charlotte.

Jeffrey held up his hand like a stop sign. "Charlotte."

"I'm defending you, Jeffrey!"

"I know, but we're all in this together. So let's go one at a time. Susie, what were you saying?"

Susie slumped back in her chair, folded her arms over her chest, and stuck out her lower lip. "I'm done. I've said my piece."

"What else do you have to say?"

"Nothing."

"Jeffrey?" Marisol raised her hand timidly. "Going along with what Susie said about stopped clocks, when my grandmother first came here from Mexico she lived in a little town called Clockton near Santa Barbara."

Jeffrey furrowed his brow. "I checked cities and towns all

over California and I couldn't find any place with the word clock in it on the internet."

"It's not on the internet. It's an abandoned old town, like a ghost town. Or like a clock that stopped ticking. Nobody lives there anymore. My grandmother lived there sixty years ago. I remember she told us the whole town was nothing but a clock factory and a cemetery."

Everyone in the room froze, and Jeffrey's eyes were glowing. "Can you call your grandmother and find out where that Clockton cemetery is located?"

"Use my phone," Susie said, handing it to Marisol.

Marisol dialed a number and spoke quietly into the phone. Jeffrey rubbed his hands together. "Now we're in business. Santa Barbara is close enough that it makes sense for Hermann Schmidt to have hid his treasure there, while he was living in Los Angeles. If we could just figure out which headstone the treasure map is located under! It's got to be located somewhere in these clues we have."

"Maybe you were right the first time," Charlotte said, on the edge of her chair, "about Blackbeard being the headless ghost. Maybe there's a grave at the cemetery with the name Blackbeard on it."

"Or Edward Teach," said Pablo. "That was Blackbeard's real name."

"Those are both possibilities," Jeffrey said. He took a sheet of paper and a pen and wrote the names Blackbeard and Edward Teach across the top. "Who else? Who else could be a headless ghost?"

"The French Revolution," Susie said. "The socialists murdered thousands of people by chopping off their heads."

"Good idea, Susie," Jeffrey said. "What was that king's name?"

"King Done Lost," said Pablo.

Jeffrey blinked. "King Done Lost?"

"King done lost his head."

Jeffrey laughed.

Charlotte, sitting tensely, was not amused. "This isn't a time for jokes," she said.

Pablo looked at her, surprised.

"King Louis XVI," Susie said. "That was the king. And Marie Antoinette."

Jeffrey added their names to the list. "Who else?"

"General Custer," Pablo said. "He didn't lose his head, but he lost his scalp."

Jeffrey laughed and wrote Custer's name down. Charlotte sighed loudly and shook her head.

Marisol clicked off the phone and handed it back to Susie. "My grandmother didn't have the address to the cemetery, but she told me how to get to old Clockton. She said we couldn't miss finding the cemetery if it's still there. She said the whole town was the size of a postage stamp."

"Excellent work, Marisol," Jeffrey said.

Marisol smiled and patted Susie on the arm. "Susie gave me the idea."

Pablo suddenly leapt to his feet. "Whoa! Jeffrey, I just had an idea! Where's your Bible?"

Jeffrey gave him a quizzical look, and motioned at the bookcase. Pablo made a beeline for it and ran his finger along the titles, talking all the while. "It says *see kings*, right? *See kings plunder the headless ghost*? Well, Kings is a book in the Bible. So let's see Kings."

Jeffrey shot straight up in his chair. "Pablo, it's brilliant!"

Pablo found Jeffrey's Douay-Rheims Bible and pulled it free of the bookcase. He flipped through the pages, found the chapter he wanted, and skimmed through it, running his finger down the page. The others watched him, waiting.

Pablo jabbed the book with his finger. "Whoa! Jeffrey, I think this it! It's Kings, Chapter 17, David and Goliath." Pablo began to read: "*And when the Philistine arose and was coming, and drew nigh to meet David, David made haste, and ran to the fight to meet the Philistine.*"

Marisol popped out of her chair and stood next to him, leaning over his shoulder and following along as Pablo read from the Bible and ran his finger along the lines. "*And he put his hand into his scrip, and took a stone, and cast it with his sling, and fetching it about struck the Philistine in the forehead. And the stone was fixed in his forehead: and he fell on his face upon the earth.*"

Pablo glanced up from the Bible. "Now check this out: *He ran, and stood over the Philistine, and took his sword, and drew it out of the sheath, and slew him, and cut off his head. And listen to this: And David taking the head of the Philistine brought it to Jerusalem.*"

Pablo slammed the book shut so hard it boomed. "The headless ghost! And David became a king, remember? King David! *See kings plunder the headless ghost*! It all fits! Goliath is the headless ghost!"

"Whoa," said Marisol.

"Double whoa," said Susie.

Jeffrey grabbed his paper and wrote GOLIATH in big block letters across the top. He looked up and his eyes were gleaming. "I think we got it," he said. "Somewhere in the Clockton cemetery is a grave marked Goliath, or one of these other names. Under that grave's headstone is a map to the treasure."

"When do we go?" Pablo asked.

"Right now!" said Charlotte.

"It's six o'clock," Susie told her, "and dark outside. By the time we get there it'll be really late."

"You're right, Susie," Jeffrey said. "It's too late to go now. We'll go tomorrow, first thing after school. I'll look up the bus schedules."

"I got football practice," Pablo said.

"And I have cheer practice," Marisol said.

149

Charlotte stared at them in disbelief. "This is a treasure worth millions of dollars and you're worried about football and cheerleading?"

Four sets of eyes stared back at her.

"We have obligations," Susie said.

"I wasn't talking to you," Charlotte snapped. She turned to Jeffrey. "Can I talk to you, Jeffrey? Alone?"

The room was silent.

"Let's go upstairs," Jeffrey said.

Charlotte snatched up her purse, stalked across the room, and climbed the basement stairs, her skirt flipping defiantly behind her.

Jeffrey looked at his friends and shrugged. "I'll be right back." He rose and followed Charlotte up the stairs.

Susie turned to Pablo and Marisol with an unbelieving look. She waited until they heard the upstairs front door open, followed by Jeffrey and Charlotte stepping outside and the door closing behind them, and then she blurted, "That girl is a – "

"Don't say it," Marisol said, holding up her hand and cutting Susie off.

"But she is!" Susie insisted.

"That might be true," Marisol said, "but she's Jeffrey's friend." Marisol paused for a moment to let the importance of what she was about to say next sink in. "And I think Jeffrey's in love."

"*What?!*"

"I'm serious," Marisol said. "Have you seen the way he looks at her? His whole face lights up. Look at the way he cleaned this room. And that shirt he's wearing. Yup, Jeffrey's in love."

"Jeffrey, the doughboy?" Susie said in astonishment. "It *is* the end of the world as we know it."

Pablo noticed Marisol watching him with a curious eye. "What?" he asked.

"Nothing," she said, blushing and turning away.

Pablo turned to Susie. She was watching him, too. "What?"

"Nothing!" Susie leaned over and whispered in Marisol's ear.

"What?" Pablo demanded of them both.

"Nothing!" they both shot back.

◆◆◆◆◆

Outside, night had fallen. Jeffrey and Charlotte stood just outside the front door, illuminated by a dim porch light.

"I'm sorry about the scene I made downstairs," Charlotte said. "But you can see my point, can't you? I mean, you're way smarter than your friends."

"They're smart, too," Jeffrey said.

"Not like you."

"We can go for the treasure on Saturday," he said. "We'll

have all day."

"By then it might be too late!" She faced him squarely. "Let's go tonight, Jeffrey."

"In the dark like this? It would be too hard."

"Don't you want that money? It's our money! And we can keep all of it."

"That's crazy," Jeffrey said. "And it would never work."

"Why not?" Charlotte asked, her voice shaky.

"Two reasons. First, how would we spend the treasure, or turn it into money? You can't just walk into a bank with a five-hundred-year-old gold coin and say, 'Cash this in.' And then there's the moral issue. I don't want that fat man to get it, but is it really ours to keep?"

"Gold can be melted down," Charlotte explained. "Plus there are collectors and places to go that will buy gold coins, no questions asked. I know how to find them. And museums. People think museums are these wonderful places, but they buy artifacts that they know are stolen all the time. As for your second point, it's a dead man's treasure, Jeffrey. It belongs to whoever finds it."

"How do you know all this?" Jeffrey asked.

"I just know."

She seized Jeffrey by the arm, her eyes alive and dangerous. "Let's get the treasure, Jeffrey! Tonight! Just you and me! And then we'll run away! We'll have millions of dollars! We can go wherever we want! Do whatever we want!"

"Are you serious?"

"Yes, I'm serious, can't you see? Please, Jeffrey, I need you for this."

"I can't run away," he stammered. "My family is here. My life is here. What about your dad?"

She released his arm and lowered her eyes. "My dad is a louse."

"He's still your dad."

"You don't understand." She looked into his face with pleading eyes. "Let's get the treasure! We can do it! I know we can do it! Please, Jeffrey!"

"I can't, Charlotte. Pablo's my best friend. And Marisol – "

"I'm your friend, too." She took his arm again and tears welled in her eyes. "Please don't make me go back to my dad."

"What's wrong with your dad?"

Charlotte cast her eyes downward and shook her head.

"You can tell me," Jeffrey said.

She shook her head again and stepped away from him. "I have to go," she said quietly.

"Come with us on Saturday," Jeffrey insisted. "We'll find the treasure together."

She turned away from him. "Goodbye, Jeffrey."

"Charlotte, wait." He took a step towards her. She walked

quickly off the porch, dabbing her eyes and refusing to look at him.

"Charlotte!"

She broke into a run, down the sidewalk and across neighboring lawns. Jeffrey watched until he could no longer see her. He stood alone in front of his house, his hands trembling and his heart thumping against his chest.

On her own and out of sight, Charlotte saw a man ahead of her on the sidewalk and slowed to a walk. As she drew closer, the man became clearer. It was Markus.

He positioned himself in the middle of the sidewalk, blocking her path. "Hey," he said. Charlotte avoided his eyes and tried stepping past him. "Hey!" he repeated, and grabbed for her arm. Charlotte pulled free, but Markus reached around her and pinned both her arms. "Stop it!" she cried. He dragged her to a black sedan, parked at the curb.

Markus opened the door to the back seat and shoved Charlotte inside. He piled into the car after her and slammed the door shut. In the front seat, perched behind the wheel, sat the fat man. He glanced up at Charlotte in the rear view mirror. "What did they tell you?"

"Nothing!"

Markus slapped her hard across the face. Charlotte screamed. "Talk!" Marcus ordered. Charlotte shook her head. Marcus slapped her again. Charlotte shrieked and covered her face.

"I ask you again, Charlotte," said the fat man. "What did they tell you?"

Charlotte cowered against the car door, whimpering. Markus raised his hand. "Don't!" Charlotte cried.

"Then talk," Markus warned, his hand still raised.

"I know where it is!" Charlotte said, gushing between sobs.

The fat man turned around and stared at her from the front seat. "The treasure?"

"Yes, the treasure! I know where it is!"

Markus, his hand poised to strike, looked to the fat man. The fat man shook his head no, and turned back around in the front seat.

Charlotte huddled in the corner of the back seat, crying softly. Markus settled back in his seat, watching her with a smirk. The fat man turned the ignition key and started the car.

Chapter 25

"She's mad, huh, Jeffrey?" Pablo said.

"Yeah, she's mad." Though he was back downstairs with his friends, Jeffrey's mind was a million miles away. He sat in his beanbag chair and thought about Charlotte's words and the look in her eye. It was Marisol who spoke and brought him back to life.

"Is Charlotte rich?" she asked.

"I don't think so," Jeffrey replied, his mind still murky. "When we first met her, she said she needed the fifty dollars of reward money we offered her. Why do you ask?"

"Because that bag she had is one that I've seen in fashion magazines. It's expensive."

"Those shoes she was wearing are expensive, too," said Susie. "I can't afford them."

Jeffrey nodded and stared absently at the wall, his mind churning. Charlotte's bag, her shoes ... something tugged at the back of his mind. What was it? *What was it?*

His friends watched, and waited. "How long is he going to sit there like that?" Susie asked.

Pablo shrugged. "Maybe an hour. Maybe more."

"*What?*"

"He's thinking," was all Pablo said.

"About what, food?"

"Don't disturb a sleeping genius," Marisol said.

Susie spun around in her chair. "Don't you start, Marisol. Genius, my you-know-what."

"Jeffrey's smart," Marisol said.

"So am I, but I don't sit like a zombie, drooling and staring at the wall."

"He's not drooling," Pablo said.

"He might as well be." Susie popped out of her chair, walked over to Jeffrey, and passed her hand slowly in front of his face. Jeffrey didn't blink. "He's in a coma!" Susie exclaimed.

"Shhh," Pablo cautioned. "Don't bother Jeffrey when he's thinking."

"If he's thinking, I'm leaving. Come on, Marisol." She took Marisol by the arm and pulled her out of her chair. The two girls started for the basement steps. "Are you coming, Pablo?" Susie called back.

"I'll be up later," Pablo replied. He knew Jeffrey was on the verge of a discovery about the case and he wanted to be the first to hear it.

"We'll be at my house," Marisol said, and she and Susie climbed the basement stairs.

Jeffrey blinked and swung around in his beanbag chair, an abrupt urgency to his voice. "Marisol? Where's Marisol?"

"Here!" Marisol called from the top of the stairs.

"Marisol, come here!" Jeffrey shouted.

Marisol clamored down the basement stairs with Susie close behind her. She found Jeffrey with a wild look in his eye. "Marisol, when the fat man had us all tied up, what did he say in German over the phone?"

"He said he was going to make us all talk," Marisol said.

"Make who talk?"

"Us."

"Give me his exact words."

"I don't remember."

"Think! Think hard! It's important!" Jeffrey was on the edge of his chair, and now so was Pablo. The girls were tense and excited.

"He said ..." Marisol paused, her mind drifting back. "He said he had four kids that he thought were spies and he was going to make them talk."

Jeffrey snapped his fingers. "That's it!"

"What's it," Susie asked.

"He said four kids. Four. But there were five of us, remember? The four of us, plus Charlotte. Why didn't he say five kids?"

Pablo's voice was shaky. "Because he meant us, not Charlotte?"

"Exactly."

Susie turned to Marisol. "Are you sure he said four kids?"

"Yes, yes, I'm certain now that I remember. He said 'vier', which is German for four. Four kids."

Jeffrey popped out of his chair. "He said four kids, because he wasn't going to make Charlotte talk, only us. She was a plant."

"What's a plant?" Susie asked.

"A spy. A stooge. That night we first met her, she told me she'd heard about us from our last case. She knew who we were and when she heard we were looking for the gray Porsche, she led us to the fat man on purpose, thinking we knew something about the treasure."

"She lied to us?" Marisol said.

"Yes, she lied. To all of us. Especially me. Tonight she talked about her father. Her father is probably Markus or the fat man."

The girls gasped.

"Isn't that Markus a cop?" Pablo asked.

Jeffrey scoffed. "He's not a cop. If he is, he's crooked. He's probably a German citizen, a mercenary like the fat man, out to betray his own people." He smacked himself in the forehead with the palm of his hand. "How could I be so stupid?"

"It's okay, Jeffrey," Marisol said. "She had us all fooled."

"It's not okay! She knows everything. They could be on their way to the Clockton cemetery right now!" He faced his friends. They eyed him back curiously. "We've got to go for that treasure," he said. "We've got to go now."

"Now?" Susie said. "It's dark outside, it's almost seven

o'clock. By the time we get there, it'll be ten o'clock. And how are we going to get there?"

"What if we skip school tomorrow," Pablo suggested, "and leave early in the morning?"

Jeffrey shook his head. "For all we know, Charlotte, the fat man, and Markus are all headed there right now. By tomorrow, the treasure could be gone."

"Shouldn't we call the police?" Susie asked.

"They'll think we're crazy," Jeffrey said, "and there's no way they'll go out to that cemetery tonight. But the time they act on this, it'll be too late. We'll call them once we're home here with the treasure."

"It sounds dangerous."

"We'll quit at the first sign of danger. If we're lucky, they won't start out till morning, and by then we'll be home with the treasure. But don't you see? We have to go now. We owe it to the people of Germany, and to the people the fat man has killed. If he gets his hands on that treasure, he's won."

Pablo, Marisol and Susie all looked at each other. "We'll have to call our parents with some story and tell them we'll be home late," Susie said. Marisol gave Pablo a small nod, and Pablo turned to Jeffrey. "Let's go."

Jeffrey grabbed the basement phone and punched in a number. When the line picked up, he spoke breathlessly. "Hello, Mr. Beasley? It's Jeffrey Jones."

Chapter 26

"Highly irregular, I tell you. Highly irregular."

Mr. Beasley drove steadily through the night. His left leg was still in a cast, but his right foot was free to brake and accelerate. Pablo sat next to him in the passenger seat, a flashlight in his hands. Jeffrey, Marisol, and Susie filled the back seat, all holding flashlights.

"But it's a treasure hunt, Mr. Beasley," Pablo explained. "Remember what you said? In a treasure hunt, all propriety goes out the window."

"Indeed. But I can just imagine the uproar if anything should go wrong. I caught an earful from your fathers the last time."

"Don't worry, nothing will go wrong," Pablo said, trying his best to sound innocent. He glanced at the back seat where Jeffrey sat, staring morosely out the window.

Jeffrey had been plenty expressive on the phone with Mr. Beasley when he talked him into driving them to the Clockton cemetery, but he hadn't said two words the entire time they'd been driving. It had been left to Pablo and the girls to entertain the teacher by keeping the conversation flowing.

Of course, when Jeffrey spoke with Mr. Beasley on the phone, he conveniently left out the part about Charlotte and the fat man possibly racing to the graveyard ahead of them. So Pablo and the girls left it out, too.

"Jeffrey," Marisol whispered.

No answer.

Marisol nudged him with her elbow. "Jeffrey?"

Still no answer.

Jeffrey stared out the window with such a look of sullenness that even Mr. Beasley was concerned. "Is he all right?" he asked, gazing up at Jeffrey in the rear view mirror.

"We're never sure," said Susie.

Enormous rain drops splattered the windshield.

"Blast," said Mr. Beasley. He turned on the windshield wipers just as the deluge arrived, hammering the roof and windows.

Jeffrey continued to stare out the window, and it rained all the way to the cemetery.

◆◆◆◆◆

It was after ten o'clock and the rain had stopped when they finally reached the abandoned Clockton cemetery. An eight foot high brick wall surrounded the property, and what looked like it had once been an entrance was gated, chained, and secured with a heavy padlock. They puttered past the entrance about fifty yards before Jeffrey finally spoke. "Let us out here, Mr. Beasley. We'll climb the wall."

Mr. Beasley pulled the car over, killed the engine, and

turned off the headlights. The night outside was inky black. "You know if it wasn't for my leg, I'd go with you," he said.

"Sure, we know, Mr. Beasley," said Pablo. "Give us an hour. If we can't find the treasure by then, we'll come back." He opened the car door and stepped outside, his breath frosting in the forty-degree air. Jeffrey and the girls climbed out of the back seat.

"Promise me you'll be careful," Mr. Beasley said.

"We will," said Pablo, before closing the car door.

Mr. Beasley leaned over the car seat and lowered the window on the passenger door. "Which one of you has the phone?"

"I do," said Susie.

"Call me if you need anything."

"I will."

Mr. Beasley watched as Jeffrey and his friends approached the imposing eight foot wall. "Be careful scaling that wall!" he called out.

Pablo gave Mr. Beasley a thumbs-up. Then he and Jeffrey stood sideways to the wall and laced their fingers together. Marisol put a hand on each of their shoulders and stepped into their laced fingers. They boosted her up and she climbed atop the wall and sat there while the boys boosted Susie up alongside of her. Then both girls lowered themselves down on the other side, hanging from their hands and dropping the rest of the way.

Pablo laced his own fingers together and gave Jeffrey a shaky lift up. "Do you need a hand?" Jeffrey asked from atop the wall.

"No, I'm okay," Pablo said.

Jeffrey nodded. Hanging onto the top of the wall, he lowered himself clumsily down the other side until his arms were fully extended and then dropped the remaining distance. His feet hit the ground and his body crumpled, landing with an ugly splat.

"Smooth, Jeffrey," Susie said. "Real smooth."

Pablo hoisted himself up to the top of the wall, gave a final wave to Mr. Beasley, and dropped down on the other side.

Mr. Beasley, still leaning across the car seat, called out the open passenger window, "For God's sakes, watch out for each other," but they were up and over the wall and beyond the hearing of his voice.

Chapter 27

Four flashlight beams cut through the dark. Jeffrey led his friends into the cemetery. They stepped past naked trees and over a carpet of dead leaves that cracked and crumbled under their shoes. It smelled of cold earth and rotting wood crucifixes. Before them, in sad disrepair, lay thousands of headstones and monuments.

Susie cast her flashlight beam in a wide arc. "Look at all these graves! How in the world are we going to find the one we want?"

"Well, we have to start somewhere," Jeffrey said. "There are four of us and we each have a flashlight. If we split up we'll be able to cover more ground."

Susie gave him a horrified look. "I'm not walking around a graveyard at night by myself!"

"Me, neither," said Marisol. "It's scary here."

"All right," Jeffrey conceded. "We'll split into two groups. If either team finds anything, give a shout and wave your flashlight beam in the air."

Susie frowned. "Don't tell me I have to team up with you."

"You're the one who complained about being alone!"

Marisol grinned impishly. "Yeah, Susie, this is an investigation, not a high school dance."

Pablo laughed. Susie spun on her heel. "Don't you start,

Marisol!"

"Come on," Jeffrey barked. "We're wasting time." He waved his flashlight at Susie as an indication for her to follow him, and started off. Susie gave Jeffrey a mock salute, drawing laughs from Pablo and Marisol, and fell in step behind him.

Pablo felt a breeze flutter over his face. He turned his head to it. Light drops of icy cold precipitation fell over his cheeks. To the west lay the Pacific Ocean and with it came a heavy mist and the smell of salt water.

"What is it?" Marisol asked.

"Fog," Pablo answered. "Looks like a heavy one, too." He cupped his hands at the sides of his mouth and shouted. "Jeffrey!"

Across the cemetery, Jeffrey stopped and turned.

Pablo pointed his flashlight westward. "Fog's rolling in!"

Jeffrey glanced toward the ocean, and then watched as a haze blew in over Pablo and Marisol. He blinked his flashlight at them as a sign that he understood, but in seconds his friends were covered in mist and disappeared from view.

"What does that mean, fog's rolling in?" asked Susie, at his side.

"It means we have to move fast," Jeffrey told her, "before we lose all visibility."

"Great," Susie said. "We're going to end up lost in a

cemetery at night."

"Speak for yourself," said Jeffrey.

They faced a double row of graves. Jeffrey pointed with his flashlight. "You take that side, I'll take this one. Look for a headstone with the name Goliath. And keep those other names in mind, too."

"I know, I know."

They ventured down the row of graves, shadows moving in the dark. The fog came fast. Within minutes they were covered in mist, unable to see beyond one or two feet in front of them.

"See anything?" Jeffrey called.

"No. Do you?" Susie called back.

"Not yet. Keep looking."

"Yeah, right. Why do I waste my time with you, Jeffrey Jones?"

Jeffrey bristled, but didn't respond.

Across the graveyard, Pablo and Marisol made their own way through the fog. They passed row after row of graves, shining their flashlight beams across the headstones and monuments.

They couldn't see one another, but they heard each other's footsteps crunching in the dark, and they could hear each other's panted breaths, even as their own breath frosted in front of them.

"Do you think these dead people mind us being here?"

Marisol's voice called.

"Nah," Pablo called back. "They don't mind. These people haven't had any excitement in years."

Marisol giggled.

"What?" Pablo said.

"This grave I'm looking at. The name says Ima Right. Get it?"

"Ha! You know what her husband's name is?"

"What?"

"Ura Wrong."

Marisol laughed.

They started down another long row of graves.

"Pablo, where are you?"

"Over here." He flashed his light in the direction where her voice had come.

"Don't wander away from me."

"I won't."

Jeffrey and Susie continued their quest.

"What if we don't find this grave?" Susie asked.

"We'll find it."

"How do you know?"

"Because I know."

"Jeffrey Jones, all knowing and all wise."

"That's right."

Susie shrieked.

Jeffrey's heart jumped. He spun around, fumbling with his flashlight and swinging its beam around in the dark. "What is it?"

"Nothing. I tripped."

"Well, pay attention to where you're going!" he snapped, angry at the momentary scare she gave him.

He didn't see Susie's tongue, sticking out at him, in the dark.

Far across the cemetery and alone in the dark, Pablo and Marisol worked their way down a gentle slope.

"Pablo?"

"Yeah?"

"Can I ask you something?"

"Sure."

"Promise you won't laugh?"

"No."

"Pablo!"

"Alright, I guess so."

"No 'you guess so'! You have to promise me."

"Okay. I promise."

The night was silent.

"What's the question?"

"Do you think I'm pretty?"

Marisol stood in front of a grave, surrounded by fog, barely breathing. Her heart thudded against her chest as she waited for Pablo's response.

Finally, his voice came. "You're better than pretty. You're beautiful."

Alone in the dark, Marisol's face glowed.

A twig snapped in the darkness behind her and her smile vanished. She turned sharply and listened. A faint rustling sound came from the brush below her, followed by an oily smell that oozed up into her nostrils. She trained her flashlight on the overgrown grass and watched as it swayed, curled, and flattened. Something was alive and headed her way!

And then she saw it: the large brown head of a snake, followed by its four foot long body. It slithered on its belly out of the grass and over the top of her canvas sneakers. Marisol felt the weight and warmth of the snake's body as it slid across her shoes. She watched, her eyes wide open, and then she screamed.

She leapt back several feet and collided with Pablo. They stumbled and fell to the ground, landing on top of a grave. "A snake!" Marisol cried.

"Where?"

"There!" she pointed.

Pablo aimed his flashlight, but the slimy serpent had disappeared.

Marisol shuddered and snuggled against him. Pablo laid his flashlight on the ground next to them and wrapped his arms around her. They clung to each other, feeling the warmth of each other's bodies.

Pablo looked up and saw his flashlight beam illuminating a crumbling headstone in front of them. He stared at it and blinked his eyes. "Hey," he said, half to himself and half to Marisol. "Hey!"

Marisol unfurled her body and lifted her head. Pablo pointed at the headstone in front of them. "Look!"

Marisol craned her neck and read the inscription on the headstone: "Frances Hugo Lieth Here. 1898-1931."

"Look at his last name," Pablo said.

"Hugo."

"Now look at the next word."

"Lieth."

"Hugo lieth," Pablo said. "Go-lieth. Get it?"

Marisol shot up to a seated position and stared at the headstone, barely breathing.

◆◆◆◆◆

Jeffrey and Susie finished a long double row of graves and started on another, swinging their flashlight beams over an endless parade of headstones.

"Are you going to tell me what happened between you and that Charlotte?" Susie asked.

"Nothing happened."

"Ho! You wish it did. I know you liked her."

Jeffrey didn't respond.

"Can you hear me, Jeffrey?"

"No."

"Fine, be that way. But don't you want to talk about it? I mean, you don't have to tell me, but you can tell me if you want to. 'Cause even though you don't have to, if you really want to, it's okay. So do you want to?"

He felt his face begin to flush and was thankful she couldn't see him. "No," he said.

"Are you sure?"

Jeffrey bounced his flashlight beam across an old marble headstone and considered her offer. Charlotte's betrayal cut like a dagger into his heart. Alone in the dark, unable to see Susie, but able to hear her voice in the night, a part of him felt like opening up.

Susie prodded him. "If you don't want to, it's okay. But if you do want to, you can. I won't make fun of you."

He thought about Charlotte, the way she had deceived them all, especially him, and his voice came out shaky. "She lied to me."

"What did she say? What did you guys talk about when you went upstairs?"

"She wanted us to find the treasure together and run away."

Silence, and then: "Was she serious?"

"I think so." His voice choked and he fought to steady it.

"But it's all over now. I'm sure she's telling that fat man where the treasure is."

"Gone with the wind, huh, Jeffrey? Oh well, looks like you're stuck with me."

Jeffrey froze. Did Susie just say what he thought she said?

"What?" he said.

"What?" she said.

"What did you just say?"

"Nothing."

"No, you just said something. What was it?"

"Nothing, I said nothing. I'm an impartial observer, remember? A speck of dust on the table of life; wandering through a graveyard in the dead of night, looking for some ancient treasure that probably doesn't exist. That's me, a wandering, meaningless, nomad of nothing."

Jeffrey found himself laughing. Susie joined him. Their laughter was interrupted by distant cries, calling to them across the dark, fog-enshrouded graveyard.

Susie snapped to attention, her voice low and awed. "It's Pablo and Marisol. They must have found something."

Jeffrey felt the hair on the back of his neck rising up. In an instant, he was running blindly through the fog, dodging headstones and leaping over graves.

"Wait!" Susie cried. Racing, she caught up with him and reached for his hand. Together they ran, neither letting go until just before they reached their friends, standing by the headstone they'd found.

Pablo was breathless with excitement. "Jeffrey, look at this!" He pointed his flashlight beam at the inscription on the headstone. "Hugo lieth," he said. "Go-lieth."

Jeffrey bent down to read the inscription. "Pablo, you're right!"

"We didn't look under the headstone yet," Marisol said. "We were waiting for you."

Jeffrey fell to his knees and ran his hand along the base of the headstone. Finding a small crevice, he slipped his hand inside. His fingers touched paper and his voice jumped. "I found it!"

Pablo and the girls crowded around him. Jeffrey tried to extract the paper brushing against his fingertips, but his hand was wedged in so tight he couldn't open his fingers to grasp it. "My hand's too big."

"Let me try," said Marisol.

Jeffrey twisted his hand like a corkscrew and pulled it free, wincing as the rough stone scraped against his flesh.

He scooted aside and Marisol knelt next to him. She had small delicate hands, and she slid one of them into the crevice and grasped the paper that Jeffrey had touched. "I got it!" she said.

Slowly, carefully, she eased her hand free of the crevice. Clasped between her fingers was a worn, yellowed envelope.

Susie gasped. Pablo stared at the envelope. "You open it,

Jeffrey," Marisol said, handing him the envelope.

With trembling fingers, Jeffrey opened the envelope flap and extracted a sheet of paper folded in thirds. The paper was as worn and yellowed as the envelope. Marisol leaned in close, and Pablo and Susie crowded in behind them, shining their flashlights down on the paper in Jeffrey's hands.

Jeffrey unfolded the paper and read aloud a single word: "Nein."

"What?" Pablo took a step back.

"No way!" Susie groaned.

"That's not the map?" Marisol asked, staring at the paper.

Jeffrey scowled. "It's a taunt. A taunt from a dead man." He crumpled the paper into a ball and threw it as far as he could.

"What do we do now?" Susie asked, all the life drained out of her voice.

"We think!" Jeffrey said forcefully. "We know we're close, we just have to solve the final part of the puzzle." He patted his pockets. "Does anyone have their copy of the treasure clues?"

"I do," Marisol said. She pulled a rumpled paper from her pocket and read aloud. "*I am a hidden room. Approach my outer walls, find nothing. Look within. See kings plunder the headless ghost. One step beyond the grave.*" She lowered the paper and looked at the others.

"I'm stumped," Susie said.

"Me too," said Pablo.

A bolt of fear shot through Jeffrey's veins. His usually sharp mind was suddenly as cloudy as the fog that encircled them. He'd been betrayed. Betrayed by a girl that he liked and one that took him for a fool. Had she paralyzed his ability to think?

All his life, Jeffrey had been made fun of because of his body, his clumsiness, and his glasses. His mind was all he had, and now even that was failing him, just when he needed it most. Why couldn't he think? Why?

He knew the others were depending on him and he felt their eyes watching his every move. Fumbling, he got to his feet and faced them. "Think!" he demanded, more to himself than anyone. "Think hard! If we don't find that treasure, the fat man will. He'll be rich and free instead of in jail where he belongs." He took off his glasses and rubbed his eyes. "Marisol, read those clues again."

"*I am a hidden room. Approach my outer walls, find nothing. Look within. See kings plunder the headless ghost. One step beyond the grave.*"

Pablo shrugged. Susie looked at Marisol and shook her head.

Jeffrey put his glasses back on. "That's it," he muttered. "It says, *One step beyond the grave.*" Jeffrey pointed at the neighboring headstones to their left and to their right. "That means either this grave or that grave. They're both one step away."

Pablo dove for the headstone on their right and groped frantically along its base. "Not here!"

Jeffrey ran to the headstone on their left. He found an indentation along the bottom of the stone, reached inside and pulled out another faded envelope. He ripped open the envelope and pulled out a sheet of paper. Holding his flashlight with one hand and the paper with his other, he read aloud: "*Congratulations. You're almost there.*"

Susie and Marisol whooped with joy.

"Keep going, Jeffrey," Pablo said.

Jeffrey read: "*Take twenty paces west.*"

"Which way is west?" Susie asked.

"It's this way," said Pablo, already marking off the distance. Jeffrey and the girls fell in behind him, their flashlights cutting through the fog.

Pablo marched twenty steps and stopped. "What next?"

Jeffrey read: "*Ten paces north.*"

Pablo marched, the others followed. He stopped in front of a small mound with a boulder at its head. "Now what?"

"That's all it says," Jeffrey replied.

Pablo stared down at the mound in front of him. "Then this has to be it."

Marisol stood next to Pablo. "Is it a grave?"

"We can't just dig up a grave," Susie said.

"I agree," said Jeffrey. He stepped closer, shining his

flashlight on the ground in front of them and at the barren rock at its head. "But this is just a rock; it's not a real headstone. Probably not a real grave, either." He turned and faced the others. "Do we dig or not?"

"We've come this far, I think we have to," Pablo said.

"I think so, too," said Marisol.

"Do we go home and get shovels?" Susie asked.

"There's no time," Jeffrey said. "We'll have to use our hands."

Pablo rolled up the sleeves on his jacket, got down on his knees, with his flashlight on the ground next to him, and pawed at the dirt. The others followed. High above, the wind howled through the tree tops and the moon lay hidden behind the thickening fog.

♦♦♦♦♦

Back at the car, Mr. Beasley waited. He turned on the car radio, tuned it to a classical music station, and adjusted the volume to a soft tone. Blissful now, he nestled back into the plush leather seat and smiled.

Eyes closed, immersed in the music of the masters, he neither saw nor heard the dark sedan that pulled up silently fifty yards behind him and turned off its lights.

Chapter 28

The graveyard lay blanketed by a dull gray mist that hung over it like a death shroud. With it, came a cold, biting wind and an eerie sense of impending doom.

Illuminated by their flashlights on the ground next to them, Jeffrey and his friends kneeled in the dirt, pawing and clawing their way into the ground, like dogs digging for a bone. Thirty minutes later, their hands struck wood.

"Is it a coffin?" Marisol asked.

"Don't know yet," Pablo answered.

"It's not very deep for a coffin," Jeffrey observed.

"I don't think it is a coffin," Susie said. "I think it's something else."

Excited now, they dug deeper and faster, burrowing into the earth. Dirt covered their hands and caked in hard under their fingernails; dirt stained their clothes and smeared their faces; they inhaled dirt in their nostrils and tasted dirt in the back of their mouths. None of them cared.

In another ten minutes, they'd cleared the top of the wooden object and found it to be three feet long and two feet wide. "If it's a coffin, it must be a kid's coffin," Pablo said.

Susie recoiled. "That's terrible!"

"I'm just sayin'," Pablo replied. He rapped his knuckles on the top of the object. "Anybody in there?"

The girls shrieked.

"Keep digging," said Jeffrey.

They dug deeper around the object. It looked to be a wooden chest about two feet high.

"Let's lift it," Jeffrey said. He and Pablo took hold of the ends and pulled. The chest hardly moved.

"Too heavy," Pablo said. "It's still caked in at the bottom."

They dug deeper until they reached the bottom of the chest and got ready to try again. The girls moved aside and the boys took hold of the chest, each holding an end. "On three," Pablo said. "One, two – "

He and Jeffrey pulled with all their might. The chest rose slowly, very slowly, and then lifted free of the mud with a sucking sound. They lifted it high enough to clear the hole they'd dug and dropped it on level ground with a heavy thud.

For a moment, the four of them stood around the chest and stared down at it. "I'm afraid to look inside," Susie said.

Jeffrey knelt before the chest and yanked on a rusty padlock that jangled.

Pablo picked up the rock at the head of the mound. "Maybe that's what this is for." He hoisted the boulder, raised it high, and brought it down with a smash on the padlock. Flecks of dust and stone flew, but the lock remained.

Pablo raised the rock and brought it down twice more. On the third smash, the old lock gave way. Jeffrey unfastened it and tossed it aside. Pablo dropped the rock and knelt next to him. The girls crowded in behind them, flashlights in hand. The glow from their flashlight beams formed a circle of light that illuminated the top of the chest and the trembling hands of the two boys and left everything else in darkness.

Jeffrey and Pablo raised the chest's lid. It opened with a loud creaking of hinges. Before them lay a fortune in ancient gold coins.

For a long moment, nobody spoke. It was as if the treasure chest that lay before them and the gold within it wasn't real, but merely a distant dream, as misty and ethereal as the fog that surrounded them. Finally, Jeffrey whispered, "The lost treasure of Hernan Cortez."

Powerful military flashlight beams cut through the fog, blinding them. "Don't move!" a voice called. Striding in from the mist, came Markus and the fat man, holding guns, flashlights and shovels. "Get away from that chest!" Markus ordered.

Jeffrey and his friends raised their hands and staggered back. The fat man took their place and kneeled by the open chest. He ran his stubby fingers over the coins, their golden color shimmering and reflecting back in his spectacles. "It is the treasure," he whispered.

"What about them?" Markus asked, his Glock 17 handgun trained on Jeffrey and his friends.

The fat man looked up and Markus nodded at the young

captives. The fat man smiled. "We reward them for finding the treasure."

Markus grinned. He stepped forward and dropped a pair of shovels at the feet of Jeffrey and Pablo.

The fat man rose shakily and his eyes glistened behind his spectacles. "Dig," he ordered.

"Dig what?" Pablo wanted to know.

"A hole, big enough for four graves."

Chapter 29

So this was how he was going to die.

Mr. Beasley lay sprawled on his stomach across the front seat of his car, tied and unable to lift his head. The harsh rope fibers bit into his skin, leaving his wrists, right ankle and neck torn and raw. The gag over his mouth pulled his face back in a horrible grimace and cut sharply at the corner of his lips, forcing a trickle of blood to roll slowly down his chin and drip onto the car seat.

Those two men had meant business. When they'd first approached the car, he'd mistaken them for custodians of the cemetery. He thought his young friends had been caught trespassing and he was fully prepared to offer the two caretakers a humorous rendition of the whole escapade as nothing more than a harmless prank. Well, the joke was on him.

They'd taken his cell phone and wallet, and left him trussed up there on the front seat.

"Do we kill him now?" the muscular one had asked.

"Not yet," the fat one had answered. "We make sure we have the treasure first. Then we come back." With a chuckle, he'd added, "We might have to make him talk."

Mr. Beasley had shuddered when he heard that remark. By all accounts, the fat man was the same one the boys had described to him when they found the old gray Porsche. He recalled what the boys told him about the corpulent criminal and his blowtorch, and the teacher's hands, which were already clammy, began to perspire even more.

He pictured the fat man opening the car door and approaching him slowly, with a leer on his face and a hissing blowtorch in his hands, and panic shot through his body. He grunted and strained at his binds till his face turned purple. It was no use. He was trapped. Trapped like a rat.

If he was lucky the two men would find the treasure they were looking for and leave without killing him. But he knew those prospects were slim. His luck had never been good, and he had seen their faces. They'd have to kill him.

He thought of his wife, Mildred, and great sadness overtook him. She'd be hysterical when she heard the news. Even worse, he thought of his young friends and their families. If the two men who'd tied him up were willing to kill him, they'd kill anybody. If only he could warn them! If only –

He heard footsteps!

A single person approaching the car ...

Was this it?

Was this the end?

Chapter 30

A graveyard at midnight is a scary place, and seems even scarier when forced at gunpoint to dig your own grave.

On a night that hung cold and dark and gray with fog, Jeffrey and Pablo dug shovelful after shovelful of dirt out of an ever-deepening hole. High above, the wind whistled through the treetops like a ghost howling with glee, and clouds covered the moon.

Marisol and Susie stood helplessly by, holding their flashlights with trembling hands. Their efforts were useless. Visibility was so poor it was like being under a sea of muddy water. It was impossible to see more than a few feet directly in front and the boys could not even make out the ends of their shovels.

Markus kept his gun trained on the boys and a sneer on his lips. The fat man kneeled in front of the treasure chest, running his greedy hands over the golden coins. His gun lay on the ground at his feet.

Jeffrey put the heel of his shoe on the lip of his shovel and wedged it into the earth. He slid his left hand down the shovel's shaft and hefted up another load of dirt. The hole was now three feet deep and five feet wide. He knew their time was short and any breath they took could be their last.

He turned to the side, lifted his shovel and deposited the

dirt it held by the side of the hole. His mind churned. He had gotten his friends into this mess, and now, if he didn't get them out, they were all going to die.

He glanced at Pablo and saw his friend digging with steely determination; his jaw set firm and his eyes like cold slits. He knew that if he could just come up with a plan, Pablo would spring into action.

The fat man closed the lid to the treasure chest, picked up his gun, and rose wobbly to his feet. "Okay," he said.

A single word, but it cut like a knife.

The girls froze and the boys stopped digging, their shovels poised in midair.

"That's enough," the man said. He waved his gun at Marisol and Susie. "Get in the hole."

The girls gasped. Jeffrey and Pablo dropped their shovels by the side of the hole. Markus smiled.

"You can't kill me," Susie said. "I have a math test tomorrow!"

"Shut up." He waved his gun at the girls and they stepped gingerly into the makeshift grave. Out of the corner of his eye, Jeffrey saw Pablo reach quietly to his side and scoop up a handful of loose dirt.

The fat man fixed Jeffrey with a penetrating stare. "You are a fat and clever boy, but now your time is up. Say goodbye to your friends." He raised his gun.

"Just a minute," Jeffrey said. "If you're going to kill us,

then I have a last request."

The fat man laughed. "A last request?"

"It's customary," Jeffrey said, "before execution."

"What request?"

"I'd like to see the treasure one last time."

"How is that going to save you?"

"It won't. But if that's the reason you're going to kill us, I'd like to see it before I go."

"I'd like to see it, too," said Pablo.

The fat man took a step back and gestured at Jeffrey with his gun. "You first; then get back in the hole."

Jeffrey stepped gingerly out of the hole. Pablo followed him, casting a wary eye on Markus, who stood close by. Jeffrey, his hands held high, walked slowly to the treasure and knelt before it. The lid opened with a creak and he stared down at the gold coins. What had appeared so brilliant only minutes before now looked dull and tarnished. His heart thumped against his chest. He was closer to the fat man, but not close enough to make a jump for his gun.

"Enough," the fat man said. "Get back in the hole."

Footsteps approached, crunching in the dark, and a flashlight beam appeared. Charlotte stepped out of the fog. She saw Jeffrey kneeling in front of the treasure chest and their eyes met.

Fury passed over the fat man's face. "I told you to wait in the car!"

Charlotte glanced around at the scene in front of her: Pablo standing by the makeshift grave, a shovel at his feet; Marisol and Susie standing in the hole with frightened looks on their faces; Markus standing close to Pablo, with his Glock trained on the boy's chest.

"What's going on?" asked Charlotte. "Why are they digging?"

"We're digging our graves," Pablo said.

Charlotte turned to the fat man. "You told me you weren't going to hurt them."

"Go back to the car," he ordered.

Markus braced. He and the fat man tightened the grips on their guns.

Charlotte's lips quivered. "You said you were going to tie them up and then call the police in the morning."

"Please, Charlotte, go back to the car. This is not for you to see."

"Dad, you can't do this!"

A flicker of hope flashed in Jeffrey's eyes. "Sir," he said to the fat man, "you can keep the treasure, we don't want it. You take the treasure and go your way, and we'll go our way."

"You think I am stupid? You go to the police."

"We won't tell anyone what happened," Jeffrey said. "You have my word."

The fat man scoffed. "Your word means nothing."

"Jeffrey's word does mean something," Charlotte said.

"He never lies."

"Go back to the car, Charlotte."

"Dad, no!"

"Go!" the man ordered. "And you," he said to Jeffrey, with a wave of his gun, "get back in the hole."

Jeffrey rose slowly to his feet. He knew he had to act now or he and his friends were all dead. Pablo braced, still holding the loose dirt in his hand.

Charlotte looked at Jeffrey and their eyes met again. "I'm sorry, Jeffrey," she said. She turned to leave, took a half step, and then whirled about, grabbing for her father's gun. Jeffrey lunged forward and grabbed the man's wrist.

Marisol and Susie screamed. Pablo hurled the handful of dirt at Markus, catching him in both eyes, and followed with a hard shove that sent the big man toppling backwards into the makeshift grave. The girls scrambled out of the hole.

The fat man backhanded Charlotte with his free hand, knocking her to the ground, and wrestled Jeffrey for the gun.

Pablo snatched up his shovel and sprang forward. He swung the shovel over Jeffrey's head and hit the fat man in the side of his head with a resounding clang. The man's gun went off, firing into the dirt.

Pablo drew the shovel back and swung it again, harder this time. It whacked the fat man square in the face, flattening his nose and fracturing his glasses. The man staggered backwards and fell to the ground.

Susie took off running, disappearing in the mist. Jeffrey grabbed Charlotte by the arm and pulled her alongside, following behind Susie. "The treasure!" Charlotte cried.

"Leave it!"

"Pablo!" Marisol screamed.

Still holding the shovel, Pablo grabbed her by the hand. Together, they ran off into the fog.

Chapter 31

They ran blindly in the dark, gunshots lashing out behind them.

Susie, in the lead, cried out, "I'm lost! Which way?"

"That way," Pablo pointed with the shovel.

"I can't see anything!"

"Neither can they."

More gunshots.

Charlotte screamed as a bullet took out her leg and dropped her to the ground.

Jeffrey knelt beside Charlotte's crumpled body and the others crouched around them. Charlotte groaned and writhed in the dirt, her leg twisted horribly behind her.

Shouts and harsh words in German came from the fog behind them. Gunfire erupted. Red sparks bit into the night.

Susie covered her head. "They're going to kill us all!"

"Don't panic," Pablo said.

Charlotte gasped and clutched at Jeffrey's arm. "Don't leave me, Jeffrey!"

"I'm right here," Jeffrey said. He turned to Pablo. "We have to get her to a hospital."

Pablo nodded grimly. He looked at Marisol. "Help, Jeffrey. You too, Susie. I'll meet you at the car." He rose up on his haunches.

Marisol grabbed at his arm. "Where are you going?"

"I'll lead them on a false trail."

"Pablo, don't!" Marisol's voice shook with emotion.

"I'll be okay. Help Jeffrey."

"I can't!"

"You have to!"

The shouts of the men grew closer.

"Hurry," Pablo said. "They're almost here!"

Jeffrey and Susie put their arms around Charlotte's shoulders and under her legs. Warm blood seeped over their hands.

Susie shuddered. "Oh God. She's bleeding bad!"

"Pablo, I can't leave you!" Marisol cried.

"Go on, I'll be right behind you." He smiled and squeezed her shoulder, and then he sprang to his feet and launched the shovel like a javelin into the fog. Seconds later, it landed with a dull clang, drawing shouts and gunfire.

"That'll throw them off," Pablo said. "Now hurry, there isn't much time." He ran into the fog and disappeared.

Marisol lunged after him. "Pablo!"

Susie caught Marisol by the arm. "Marisol, we need your help!"

Marisol looked at her friends and then at Charlotte, moaning and gasping for air. Anguish covered her face. "What do I do?"

"Keep Charlotte's leg elevated," Jeffrey said, "so she

doesn't lose any more blood."

Her hands trembling, Marisol took hold of Charlotte's ankles. The three of them lifted the wounded girl and started off. They hurried through the fog, bumping into headstones and stumbling over graves. Behind them, they heard Pablo's voice growing fainter with distance: "This way, Jeffrey!" and "Over here!" followed by shouts and more gunfire.

Further and further they went, Charlotte, now unconscious, grew heavier in their arms. The shouts of the men grew dimmer. Then the fog seemed to lift and they saw the wall surrounding the cemetery ahead of them.

"Marisol," Jeffrey panted, "you go first. We'll hand Charlotte up to you."

They reached the wall and laid Charlotte on the ground in front of it. Jeffrey and Susie put their hands together and gave Marisol a boost. She poised on top of the wall, a leg on either side.

"Come on, Susie," Jeffrey said. The two of them lifted Charlotte up to Marisol, who held onto her at the top of the wall.

"I'd better give you a boost," Jeffrey told Susie.

"No, I'd better give you a boost. You'll never make it over that wall on your own."

Susie laced her fingers together. Jeffrey stepped into her hands and she boosted him up, puffing and straining. "Why do you weigh so much, Jeffrey Jones?"

Jeffrey reached the top of the wall, next to Marisol. He reached an arm down and helped pull Susie up next to them. The three of them sat panting and catching their breath, and then the girls hopped down on the other side. Jeffrey lowered Charlotte into their arms and then lowered himself down. Mr. Beasley's car sat waiting on the street ahead of them.

Jeffrey and the two girls picked up Charlotte and carried her to the car. The shouts and gunfire had stopped and the night was eerily quiet. "Where's Pablo?" Marisol said, as they neared the car.

"He'll be here," Jeffrey assured her.

"Where's Mr. Beasley?" asked Susie. The car looked empty as they approached. They reached the passenger door and Susie shrieked. Mr. Beasley was still tied up and lying across the front seat.

They laid Charlotte in the back seat and then set to work untying Mr. Beasley. "Jones, am I glad to see you!" he exclaimed when Jeffrey removed his gag. "All of you!" They untied his binds and he nodded at Charlotte passed out in the back seat. "Who is that girl? And what's wrong with her?"

"She's been shot," Jeffrey said.

"Shot? Good heavens!"

They heard shouts and the four of them turned to see Pablo climbing over the wall. "Start the car! Start the car!" he shouted.

Mr. Beasley sat up behind the wheel and started the engine. Susie sat next to him in the passenger seat. Pablo jumped down from the wall and sprinted to the car.

Jeffrey and Marisol opened the door to the back seat and Pablo jumped inside. Marisol threw her arms around his neck. "Let's go!" he shouted, slamming the car door shut behind him. "Those guys are right behind me!"

Shouts from Markus and the fat man came from just behind the wall.

Mr. Beasley slammed his foot on the gas pedal and the car roared off, tires squealing. Inside was a mix of excited voices. "A hospital, Mr. Beasley," Jeffrey shouted above them all. "We have to get her to a hospital!"

"Right!" Mr. Beasley shouted back.

And then from Pablo, "They're after us!"

Mr. Beasley glanced up at the rearview mirror and saw the black sedan following him. "Blast!"

Jeffrey held Charlotte's hand and prayed. Pablo and Marisol kept their eyes on the black sedan behind them. "They're gaining on us!" Pablo said.

Susie turned around from the front seat. "Why are they following us if we don't have the treasure?"

"They want to kill us!" Marisol said.

"We'll see about that," said Mr. Beasley. "Hang on, everyone, I'm taking evasive action." He cut the wheel sharply, sending everyone sliding to the right side of the car.

Mr. Beasley straightened the car and floored the gas pedal.

Pablo looked out the rear window and saw the sedan cut the same turn. "They're still behind us!"

Mr. Beasley spotted the freeway entrance ramp ahead. He gunned the motor, racing parallel to the entrance ramp and then cut the wheel hard to the left, hopping a slight curb and cutting over to the ramp.

The sedan followed, cutting the same sharp swerve. Its tires screamed. The car tilted and leaned, further and further, and then spun onto its side.

Inside Mr. Beasley's car, Jeffrey and his friends watched out the back windshield as the sedan flipped itself over and over and burst into flames.

Susie and Marisol screamed.

Chapter 32

The juvenile detention hospital smelled of ammonia, disinfectant, and death. It was the last place Jeffrey wanted to be, but he knew it was the last time he'd ever see Charlotte again.

His father waited for him downstairs. For once, he hadn't yelled at Jeffrey or given him a lecture. Maybe he was saving it for later.

The sheriff's deputy, a sullen, pinch-faced woman, escorted Jeffrey down the hall to Charlotte's room and stood waiting for him in the doorway. It seemed to take an enormous effort for Charlotte to lift her head, but she managed, and when she saw it was Jeffrey, she smiled weakly. "I knew you would come," she said.

Jeffrey's heart jumped. Even in her hospital bed, with straggly hair, sallow skin, and her leg under heavy bandages, Charlotte still looked pretty.

They spoke gently, quietly. Jeffrey's time seemed to pass in the blink of an eye. Before he knew it, the stone-faced deputy was rapping at the door.

"I'll be right there," Jeffrey told her, before turning his eyes back to Charlotte.

"I knew you were smart," she said. "I knew you'd find the treasure."

"The police impounded it," he told her. "Who knows where it is now."

"In case you're wondering, I meant what I said," she told him. "About the two of us. We could have run away together."

"I'm sorry."

Charlotte looked at him and tears welled in her eyes. "I know that after I'm healed I'll be sent away for a long time. But that's okay. I'm going to take your advice and use the time to get to know God."

Jeffrey smiled.

The deputy rapped on the door again.

Jeffrey gave Charlotte a little wave and started out.

"Wait!" Charlotte called to him.

Jeffrey stopped in the doorway.

Charlotte stretched out her arm, as if to reach him from the hospital bed. "Just one thing, Jeffrey, before you go; if you're right about God and about Heaven, and I believe you are, then right now my father and my uncle are both in hell."

Jeffrey felt a tightening in his throat. He stared back at her and blinked. He didn't know what to say.

Charlotte's face grew long before his eyes and she burst into tears.

The pinch-faced deputy took Jeffrey by the arm and pulled him out of the room and down the hall, her heels clacking sharply on the marble floor. Charlotte's wails echoed down the hall behind him. He felt a suffocating sickness and his face bleached white. He didn't know if he would make it to the elevator.

The morning had brought a drenching rain, but now the sun was shining and a rainbow lay painted across the clearing sky. Stepping outside with his father, Jeffrey inhaled deeply, letting the oxygen clear his head.

Charlotte's cries haunted his thoughts, but he saw the rainbow and stopped to gaze at it. The rainbow was a gift that God gave to Noah after the flood; a symbol of his covenant to man.

He and his father drove home in silence.

♦ ♦ ♦ ♦ ♦

Pablo was waiting for him on the front porch when they arrived home. Jeffrey joined his friend, while his father went in the house. They sat for a long time, neither boy speaking a word. Finally, Pablo said, "Marisol and her mom are making dinner for us tonight. Susie will be there, too."

Jeffrey nodded.

More time passed.

A young mother pushing a stroller passed them on the sidewalk. The child in the stroller waved at them and said, "Bye-bye."

Pablo smiled at the child and waved back. He turned to Jeffrey. "Why do we teach babies to say bye-bye?"

Jeffrey stared after the stroller as it disappeared down the sidewalk. "Because for the rest of his life, the people he loves and the people he cares about will all leave him."

Pablo smiled knowingly and gave his friend a pat on the back. Together they watched the sun go down.

Thank you very much for buying this book! If you liked it, please leave a review on Amazon. You are invited to read other books in this exciting new series: The North Hollywood Detective Club In The Case of the Hollywood Art Heist

If you have a comment for me, or if you would like to join my email list and receive updates when new books in this series are released, email me at mainsmike@yahoo.com

Special thanks to Melinda W. Burt of Pixel Perfect Publishing for the cover design. And formatting. Contact her at: pixelperfectpublishing@gmail.com

In the meantime, here's a little preview of Book Three in the North Hollywood Detective Club series, available in August 2016.

The Case of the Christmas Counterfeiters

"I warned you not to interfere in my little enterprise, but you wouldn't listen. Very well, now you'll have to die."

With those words, the one-eyed man stepped out and the heavy vault door swung shut. "Wait!" cried Jeffrey Jones, but it was too late. He heard the combination lock turn. He and his two friends were locked in the airtight vault.

Pablo Reyes rushed to the inside of the vault door and grabbed the handle. He pushed, pulled, twisted, and turned, but it was no use. The door wouldn't budge. "We're stuck," he said.

"At least until somebody finds us," said Marisol Rodriguez. "I mean, eventually someone will have to find us, won't they?"

Jeffrey slumped against the side of the vault and slid down to a seated position on the floor. "It's worse than that," he said.

"What's worse?" Marisol asked.

Jeffrey felt a sick churning in his stomach. He looked up into the hopeful eyes of his young friends, but he didn't have the heart to tell them.

"What is it, Jeffrey?" Pablo asked.

"He said we have to die. That means he set the timer."

"What timer?"

"This vault comes with a safety mechanism. It's designed to go off in case of a break-in, but it's also connected to a timer in the next room. When the safety mechanism is activated, the vault is flooded with poison gas."

Marisol gasped and Pablo turned white as a sheet. An intercom buzzed and the voice of the one-eyed man crackled over a loudspeaker. "Can you hear me, boy? If you can, press the intercom button."

Jeffrey sprang to his feet and pressed the button. "I can hear you!" Pablo and Marisol crowded in close behind him. They waited for the man's response.

"I've set the timer for one hour. That's plenty of time for me to make my escape. If not, I can use your lives as leverage. Of course, at this point, I fully expect to get away. I wish I could tell you that the gas is painless, but it's not. It's excruciatingly painful. Your throat will constrict, your eyes will burn out of their sockets, and your skin will peel off. No one will save you and no one will hear you scream. Goodbye." The intercom buzzed and went dead.

Marisol screamed. Pablo jammed at the intercom button. "Hey! Hey! Come back!"

Jeffrey stared at the intercom button with a stricken look on his face. There was no way out and it was all his fault. He was going to die and his friends were going to die. He felt himself panicking and his mind went blank. How did it happen? How did they get there? Then he remembered …

The North Hollywood Detective Club in the Case of the Christmas Counterfeiters – available in November 2016

Books in the North Hollywood Detective Club Series:

-The Case of the Hollywood Art Heist

-The Case of the Dead Man's Treasure

-The Case of the Christmas Counterfeiters (November 2016)

-The Case of the Missing Valentine (February 2017)

ABOUT THE AUTHOR

Mike Mains has worked as an actor, producer, and writer in the entertainment industry. His manual "Why Films Succeed and Why They Fail" is an underground classic and the definitive guide to predicting a film's box office success.

Today, Mike pens a yearly column for Marc Lawrence's Playbook Football Preview Guide, and specializes in mystery and adventure books for young readers. He can be reached at mainsmike@yahoo.com

Made in United States
North Haven, CT
03 August 2022

22224929R00115